baseball tales

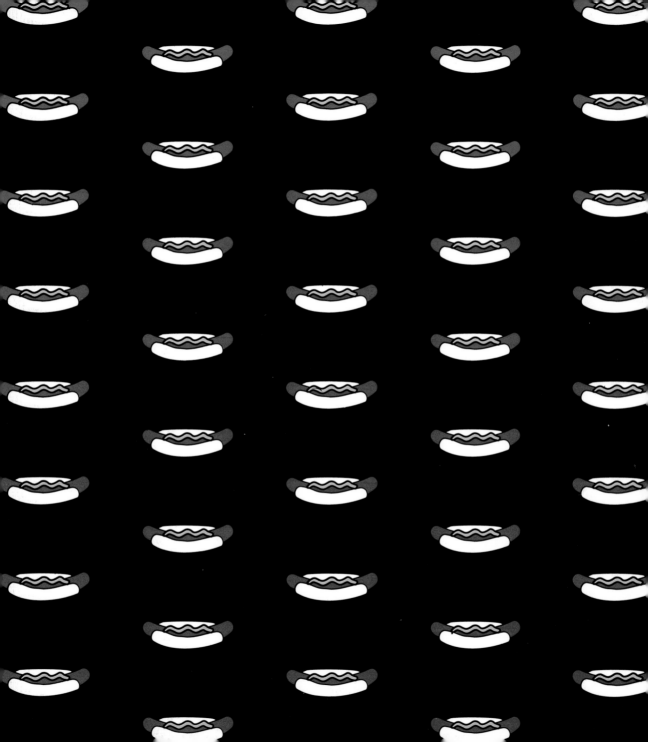

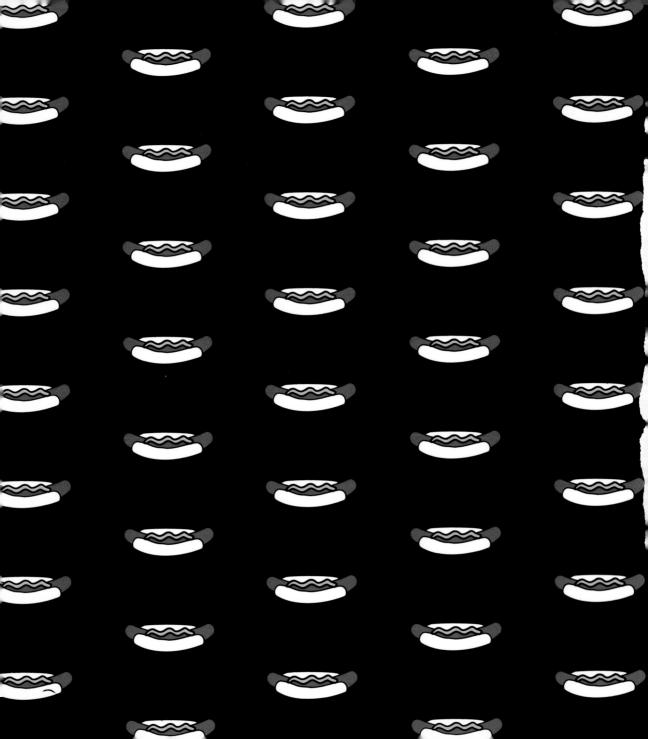

baseball tales

major league writers on the national pastime

photographs by
terry heffernan

introduction by lawrence s. ritter

VIKING
STUDIO
BOOKS

To My Outfield
Ryan, Kevin, Patrick
And Their Mom

VIKING STUDIO BOOKS
Published by the Penguin Group
Viking Penguin, a division of Penguin Books USA Inc.,
375 Hudson Street, New York 10014, U.S.A.
Penguin Books Ltd, 27 Wrights Lane, London W8 5TZ, England
Penguin Books Australia Ltd, Ringwood, Victoria, Australia
Penguin Books Canada Ltd, 10 Alcorn Avenue, Suite 300, Toronto, Ontario,
Canada M4V 3B2
Penguin Books (N.Z.) Ltd, 182-190 Wairau Road,
Auckland 10, New Zealand

Penguin Books Ltd, Registered Offices: Harmondsworth, Middlesex, England

First published in 1993 by Viking Penguin, a division of Penguin Books USA Inc.

1 3 5 7 9 10 8 6 4 2

Copyright © Fly Productions, 1993
Photographs copyright © Terry Heffernan, 1993
Introduction copyright © Lawrence S. Ritter, 1993
All rights reserved

Grateful acknowledgment is made for permission to reprint the following copyrighted works:
"How I Got My Nickname" by W. P. Kinsella from *The Thrill of the Grass* by W. P. Kinsella. Copyright © 1984 by
W. P. Kinsella. Used by permission of Viking Penguin, a division of Penguin Books USA Inc.,
and Penguin Books Canada Limited.
"You Could Look It Up" by James Thurber from *My World — and Welcome To It* by James Thurber. Copyright
1942 by James Thurber, copyright © 1970 by Helen Thurber and Rosemary A. Thurber. Reprinted by permission.
"The Rollicking God" by Nunnally Johnson. Copyright 1924 by Nunnally Johnson, copyright renewed 1952.
Reprinted by permission of Dorris Johnson.
"Baseball Hattie" by Damon Runyon from *Take It Easy* by Damon Runyon. Copyright 1936 by Hearst Magazine,
Inc.; copyright renewed © 1964 by Damon Runyon, Jr., and Mary Runyon McCann, whose copyright was assigned
to Sheldon Abend in 1992. Copyright © 1992 by Sheldon Abend.

ISBN 0-670-84700-3

CIP data available.

Printed in Japan

F Y
PRODUCTIONS

 # contents

# illustrations

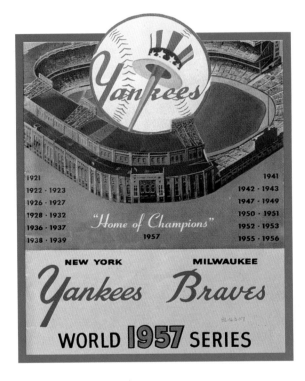

"Home of Champions"

1921	1941
1922 · 1923	1942 · 1943
1926 · 1927	1947 · 1949
1928 · 1932	1950 · 1951
1936 · 1937	1952 · 1953
1938 · 1939	1955 · 1956
1957	

NEW YORK
MILWAUKEE

Yankees *Braves*

WORLD **1957** SERIES

introduction by
l a w r e n c e   s .   r i t t e r

american poets and novelists have had a long-standing love affair with baseball. From Carl Sandburg to Marianne Moore, Thomas Wolfe to Bernard Malamud, many of this country's most renowned writers have celebrated baseball in poetry and drama. Why has this romance been so intense and lasted so long? What is so special about baseball that makes it different from other team sports? After all, basketball and hockey are faster, football is rougher and tougher, and soccer has a larger and more enthusiastic following worldwide. Nevertheless, none has the literary cheering section that baseball enjoys.

Part of the reason is the sheer beauty of the game: the desperate race to first base by a batter trying to arrive ahead of the ball; the fluid movements of an infielder digging a grounder out of the dirt and with the same motion smoothly firing it on a straight line to first base; the measured pace of an outfielder gauging the parabolic flight of a high fly ball. The same plays and movements are repeated time and again in ballgame after ballgame, and yet for baseball fans they never lose their appeal.

Writers may also be attracted to baseball by its surprising plot twists and turns — surprising because on the surface the game appears so linear and uncomplicated. Yet just about anything that happens on the field can suddenly change the direction of a game, even those plays that begin by looking routine. "Ninety feet between bases," said sportswriter Red Smith, "is the nearest to perfection that man has yet achieved."

Baseball history is replete with illustrations. In the tenth inning of the sixth game of the 1986 World Series, for example, a puny infield ground ball off the bat of Mets outfielder Mookie Wilson trickled under the glove of astonished Red Sox first baseman Bill Buckner and the Sox lost a Series they had practically won.

introduction

It was a lazy fly ball, one of a dozen that arch into the sky every day, that Giants outfielder Fred Snodgrass let slip through his hands in the tenth inning of the last game of the 1912 World Series. Fate, that time, favored the Red Sox, who won the game and the Series. The philosophically inclined Snodgrass lived for another sixty-two happy and productive years; nevertheless, when he finally passed away in 1974 nothing counted but one dreadful moment — his obituary in *The New York Times* was headlined "FRED SNODGRASS, 86, DEAD; BALLPLAYER MUFFED 1912 FLY."

Baseball consists of a succession of confrontations between two clearly identifiable individuals — the pitcher versus the batter. It is a contest of wits, intelligence, skill, and strength. It also involves courage, because the ball is as hard as a rock and often comes toward the batter at a speed approaching ninety miles an hour. At that speed, the batter has only three-tenths of a second after the ball leaves the pitcher's hand in which to judge the pitch, decide whether or not to swing (or duck!), and start moving his bat to make contact. By four-tenths of a second the ball has already smacked into the catcher's mitt.

For batters, failure is more likely than success. "Hitting a baseball is the single most difficult thing to do in all of sports," said Ted Williams, who perhaps did it better than anyone. Even Babe Ruth, the greatest baseball player of all time, hit 714 home runs but struck out almost twice as often — 1,330 times.

Bit players can steal the show. A minor character, infielder Joe Sewell, is the toughest batter to strike out in big-league history. Between 1920 and 1933, he came to bat over seven thousand times and struck out on only 114 occasions. A teammate once asked him his secret. Sewell stammered, not sure what to say. "Well," he finally answered, trying to be helpful, "you just keep your eye on the ball."

The five delightful short stories in this book demonstrate the joyous dalliance between

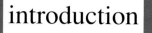

baseball and fiction. One of them, by James Thurber, is particularly distinctive in that it inspired its duplication in real life. Art often imitates life, but here is a rare case of life imitating art. Pearl du Monville, Thurber's thirty-five-inch-tall midget, appeared in the pages of *The Saturday Evening Post* in 1941. A decade later, St. Louis Browns owner Bill Veeck signed twenty-six-year-old Eddie Gaedel to a contract. Gaedel, a forty-three-inch-tall midget, came to bat as a pinch hitter against the Detroit Tigers on August 19, 1951, and walked to first base with a base on balls on four consecutive pitches — naturally, all high.

Thurber's midget got into trouble by allowing dreams of glory to dominate common sense. He swung at an easy fat pitch and hit it, but got thrown out at first base because it took him an hour to run down the baseline.

Fearful that Gaedel might succumb to the same temptation, Veeck warned him, "Eddie, I'm going to be up on the roof with a high-powered rifle, watching every move you make. If you so much as look as if you're going to swing that bat, you'll never leave this ballpark alive."

Most of these stories were written many years ago about times that are now long gone. But in baseball, the power of recollection is a great strength. One of the most vivid memories in the minds of many present-day adults is the time, long ago, when their fathers took them by the hand to their first big-league baseball game. That unforgettable ritual of childhood is unique to baseball; if it should ever disappear, the game will cease being America's national pastime.

Baseball has something other professional team sports can only envy — namely, nostalgic memories that grow ever more precious with the passage of time. "The best thing about baseball today," someone once said, "is its yesterdays."

how i got my nickname

In the summer of 1951, the summer before I was to start Grade 12, my polled Hereford calf, Simon Bolivar, won Reserve Grand Champion at the Des Moines All-Iowa Cattle Show and Summer Exposition. My family lived on a hobby-farm near Iowa City. My father, who taught classics at Coe College in Cedar Rapids, and in spite of that was still the world's number one baseball fan, said I deserved a reward — I also had a straight A average in Grade 11 and had published my first short story that spring. My father phoned his friend Robert Fitzgerald (Fitzgerald, an eminent translator, sometimes phoned my father late at night and they talked about various ways of interpreting the tougher parts of *The Iliad*) and two weeks later I found myself in Fitzgerald's spacious

by w. p. kinsella

1

country home outside of New York City, sharing the lovely old house with the Fitzgeralds, their endless supply of children, and a young writer from Georgia named Flannery O'Connor. Miss O'Connor was charming, and humorous in an understated way, and I wish I had talked to her more. About the third day I was there I admitted to being a published writer and Miss O'Connor said "You must show me some of your stories." I never did. I was seventeen, overweight, diabetic, and bad-complexioned. I alternated between being terminally shy and obnoxiously brazen. I was nearly always shy around the Fitzgeralds and Miss O'Connor. I was also terribly homesick, which made me appear more silent and outlandish than I knew I was. I suspect I am the model for Enoch Emory, the odd, lonely country boy in Miss O'Connor's novel *Wise Blood*. But that is another story.

On a muggy August morning, the first day of a Giant home stand at the Polo Grounds, I prepared to travel into New York. I politely invited Miss O'Connor to accompany me, but she, even at that early date, had to avoid sunlight and often wore her wide-brimmed straw hat, even indoors. I set off much too early and though terrified of the grimy city and shadows that seemed to lurk in every doorway, arrived at the Polo Grounds over two hours before game time. It was raining gently and I was one of about two dozen fans in the ballpark. A few players were lethargically playing catch; a coach was hitting fungos to three players in right field. I kept edging my way down the rows of seats until I was right behind the Giants dugout.

The Giants were thirteen games behind the Dodgers and the pennant race appeared all but over. A weasel-faced bat boy, probably some executive's nephew, I thought, noticed me staring wide-eyed at the players and the playing field. He curled his lip at

2

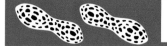

me, then stuck out his tongue. He mouthed the words "Take a picture, it'll last longer," adding something at the end that I could only assume to be uncomplimentary.

Fired by the insult I suddenly mustered all my bravado and called out "Hey, Mr. Durocher?" Leo Durocher, the Giants manager, had been standing in the third-base coach's box not looking at anything in particular. I was really impressed. That's the grand thing about baseball, I thought. Even a manager in a pennant race can take time to daydream. He didn't hear me. But the bat boy did, and stuck out his tongue again.

I was overpowered by my surroundings. Though I'd seen a lot of major league baseball I'd never been in the Polo Grounds before. The history of the place . . . "Hey, Mr. Durocher," I shouted.

Leo looked up at me with a baleful eye. He needed a shave, and the lines around the corners of his mouth looked like ruts.

"What is it, Kid?"

"Could I hit a few?" I asked hopefully, as if I was begging to stay up an extra half hour. "You know, take a little batting practice?"

"Sure, Kid. Why not?" and Leo smiled with one corner of his mouth. "We want all our fans to feel like part of the team."

From the box seat where I'd been standing, I climbed up on the roof of the dugout and Leo helped me down onto the field.

4

Leo looked down into the dugout. The rain was stopping. On the other side of the park a few of the Phillies were wandering onto the field. "Hey, George," said Leo, staring into the dugout, "throw the kid here a few pitches. Where are you from, son?"

It took me a few minutes to answer because I experienced this strange, lightheaded feeling, as if I had too much sun. "Near to Iowa City, Iowa," I managed to say in a small voice. Then "You're going to win the pennant, Mr. Durocher. I just know you are."

"Well, thanks, Kid," said Leo modestly, "we'll give it our best shot."

George was George Bamberger, a stocky rookie who had seen limited action. "Bring the kid a bat, Andy," Leo said to the bat boy. The bat boy curled his lip at me but slumped into the dugout, as Bamberger and Sal Yvars tossed the ball back and forth.

The bat boy brought me a black bat. I was totally unprepared for how heavy it was. I lugged it to the plate and stepped into the right-hand batter's box. Bamberger delivered an easy, looping, batting-practice pitch. I drilled it back up the middle.

"Pretty good, Kid," I heard Durocher say.

Bamberger threw another easy one and I fouled it off. The third pitch was a little harder. I hammered it to left.

"Curve him," said Durocher.

He curved me. Even through my thick glasses the ball looked as big as a grapefruit, illuminated like a small moon. I whacked it and it hit the right-field wall on one bounce.

"You weren't supposed to hit that one," said Sal Yvars.

"You're pretty good, Kid," shouted Durocher from the third-base box. "Give him your best stuff, George."

Over the next fifteen minutes I batted about .400 against George Bamberger, and Roger Bowman, including a homerun into the left centerfield stands. The players on the Giants bench were watching me with mild interest, often looking up from the books most of them were reading.

5

"I'm gonna put the infield out now," said Durocher. "I want you to run out some of your hits."

Boy, here I was batting against the real New York Giants. I wished I'd worn a new shirt instead of the horizontally striped red and white one I had on, which made me look heftier than I really was. Bowman threw a sidearm curve and I almost broke my back swinging at it. But he made the mistake of coming right back with the same pitch. I lopped it behind third where it landed soft as a sponge, and trickled off toward the stands — I'd seen the play hundreds of times — a stand-up double. But when I was still twenty feet from second base Eddie Stanky was waiting with the ball. "Slide!" somebody yelled, but I just skidded to a stop, stepping out of the baseline to avoid the tag. Stanky whapped me anyway, a glove to the ribs that would have made Rocky Marciano or Ezzard Charles proud.

When I got my wind back Durocher was standing, hands on hips, staring down at me.

"Why the hell didn't you slide, Kid?"

"I can't," I said, a little indignantly. "I'm diabetic, I have to avoid stuff like that. If I cut myself, or even bruise badly, it takes forever to heal."

"Oh," said Durocher. "Well, I guess that's okay then."

"You shouldn't tag people so hard," I said to Stanky. "Somebody could get hurt."

"Sorry, Kid," said Stanky. I don't think he apologized very often. I noticed that his spikes were filed. But I found later that he knew a lot about F. Scott Fitzgerald. His favorite story was "Babylon Revisited" so that gave us a lot in common; I was a real Fitzgerald fan; Stanky and I became friends though both he and Durocher argued

6

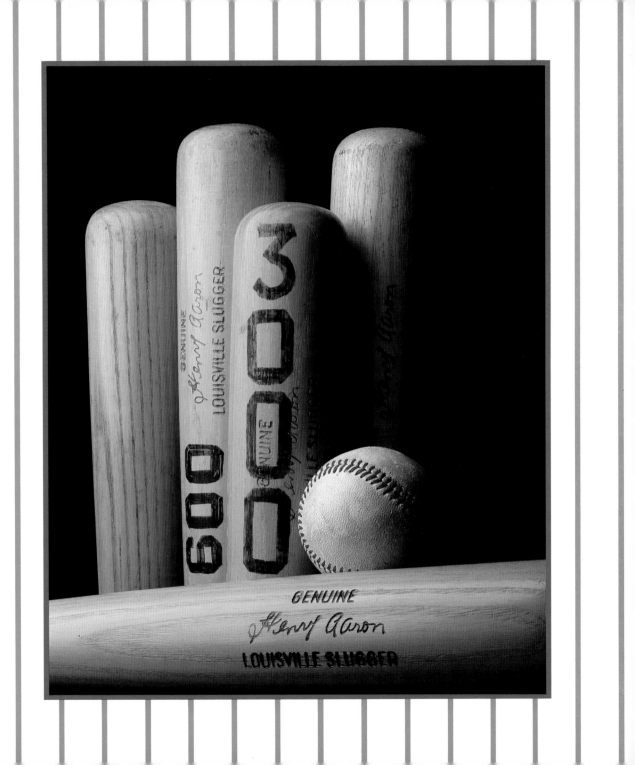

against reading *The Great Gatsby* as an allegory.

"Where'd you learn your baseball?" an overweight coach who smelled strongly of snuff, and bourbon, said to me.

"I live near Iowa City, Iowa," I said in reply.

Everyone wore question marks on their faces. I saw I'd have to elaborate. "Iowa City is within driving distance of Chicago, St. Louis, Milwaukee, and there's minor league ball in Cedar Rapids, Omaha, Kansas City. Why there's barely a weekend my dad and I don't go somewhere to watch professional baseball."

"Watch?" said Durocher.

"Well, we talk about it some too. My father is a real student of the game. Of course we only talk in Latin when we're on the road, it's a family custom."

"Latin?" said Durocher.

"Say something in Latin," said Whitey Lockman, who had wandered over from first base.

"The Etruscans have invaded all of Gaul," I said in Latin.

"Their fortress is on the banks of the river," said Bill Rigney, who had been filling in at third base.

"Velle est posse," I said.

"Where there's a will there's a way," translated Durocher.

"Drink Agri Cola . . ." I began.

"The farmer's drink," said Sal Yvars, slapping me on the back, but gently enough not to bruise me. I guess I looked a little surprised.

"Most of us are more than ballplayers," said Alvin Dark, who had joined us. "In fact

8

the average player on this squad is fluent in three languages."

"*Watch?*" said Durocher, getting us back to baseball. "You *watch* a lot of baseball, but where do you play?"

"I've never played in my life," I replied. "But I have a photographic memory. I just watch how different players hold their bat, how they stand. I try to emulate Enos Slaughter and Joe Di Maggio."

"Can you field?" said Durocher.

"No."

"No?"

"I've always just watched the hitters. I've never paid much attention to the fielders."

He stared at me as if I had spoken to him in an unfamiliar foreign language.

"Everybody fields," he said. "What position do you play?"

"I've never played," I reiterated. "My health is not very good."

"Cripes," he said, addressing the sky. "You drop a second Ted Williams on me and he tells me he can't field." Then to Alvin Dark: "Hey, Darky, throw a few with the kid here. Get him warmed up."

In the dugout Durocher pulled a thin, black glove from an equipment bag and tossed it to me. I dropped it. The glove had no discernible padding in it. The balls Dark threw hit directly on my hand, when I caught them, which was about one out of three. "Ouch!" I cried. "Don't throw so hard."

"Sorry, Kid," said Alvin Dark and threw the next one a little easier. If I really heaved I could just get the ball back to him. I have always thrown like a non-athletic girl. I could feel my hand bloating inside the thin glove. After about ten pitches, I

9

pulled my hand out. It looked as though it had been scalded.

"Don't go away, Kid," said Leo. "In fact why don't you sit in the dugout with me. What's your name, anyway?"

"W. P. Kinsella," I said.

"Your friends call you W?"

"My father calls me William, and my mother . . ." but I let my voice trail off. I didn't think Leo Durocher would want to know my mother still called me Bunny.

"Jeez," said Durocher. "You need a nickname, Kid. Bad."

"I'll work on it," I said.

I sat right beside Leo Durocher all that stifling afternoon in the Polo Grounds as the Giants swept a doubleheader from the Phils, the start of a sixteen-game streak that was to lead to the October 3, 1951, Miracle of Coogan's Bluff. I noticed right away that the Giants were all avid readers. In fact, the *New York Times* Best Seller Lists, and the *Time* and *Newsweek* lists of readable books and an occasional review were taped to the walls of the dugout. When the Giants were in the field I peeked at the covers of the books the players sometimes read between innings. Willie Mays was reading *The Cruel Sea* by Nicholas Monsarrat. Between innings Sal Maglie was deeply involved in Carson McCuller's new novel *The Ballad of the Sad Cafe.* "I sure wish we could get that Cousin Lyman to be our mascot," he said to me when he saw me eyeing the book jacket, referring to the hunchbacked dwarf who was the main character in the novel. "We need something to inspire us," he added. Alvin Dark slammed down his copy of *Requiem for a Nun* and headed for the on-deck circle.

When the second game ended, the sweaty and sagging Leo Durocher took me by the arm. "There's somebody I want you to meet, Kid," he said. Horace Stoneham's office was furnished in wine-colored leather sofas and overstuffed horsehair chairs. Stoneham sat behind an oak desk as big as the dugout, enveloped in cigar smoke.

"I've got a young fellow here I think we should sign for the stretch drive," Durocher said. "He can't field or run, but he's as pure a hitter as I've ever seen. He'll make a hell of a pinch hitter."

"I suppose you'll want a bonus?" growled Stoneham.

"I do have something in mind," I said. Even Durocher was not nearly so jovial as he had been. Both men stared coldly at me. Durocher leaned over and whispered something to Stoneham.

"How about $6,000," Stoneham said.

"What I'd really like . . ." I began.

"Alright, $10,000, but not a penny more."

"Actually I'd like to meet Bernard Malamud. I thought you could maybe invite him down to the park. Maybe get him to sign a book for me?" They both looked tremendously relieved.

"Bernie and me and this kid Salinger are having supper this evening," said Durocher. "Why don't you join us?"

"You mean J.D. Salinger?" I said.

"Jerry's a big Giant fan," he said. "The team Literary Society read *Catcher in the Rye* last month. We had a panel discussion on it for eight hours on the train to St. Louis."

Before I signed the contract I phoned my father.

11

"No reason you can't postpone your studies until the end of the season," he said. "It'll be a good experience for you. You'll gather a lot of material you can write about later. Besides, baseball players are the real readers of America."

I got my first hit off Warren Spahn, a solid single up the middle. Durocher immediately replaced me with a pinch runner. I touched Ralph Branca for a double; the ball went over Duke Snider's head, hit the wall and bounced halfway back to the infield. Anyone else would have had an inside the park homer. I wheezed into second and was replaced. I got into 38 of the final 42 games. I hit 11 for 33, and was walked four times. And hit once. That was the second time I faced Warren Spahn. He threw a swishing curve that would have gone behind me if I hadn't backed into it. I slouched off toward first holding my ribs.

"You shouldn't throw at batters like that," I shouted, "someone could get seriously hurt. I'm diabetic, you know." I'd heard that Spahn was into medical texts and interested in both human and veterinary medicine.

"Sorry," he shouted back. "If I'd known I wouldn't have thrown at you. I've got some good liniment in the clubhouse. Come see me after the game. By the way, I hear you're trying to say that *The Great Gatsby* is an allegory."

"The way I see it, it is," I said. "You see the eyes of the optometrist on the billboard are really the eyes of God looking down on a fallen world . . ."

"Alright, alright," said the umpire, Beans Reardon, "let's get on with the game. By the way, Kid, I don't think it's an allegory either. A statement on the human condition, perhaps. But not an allegory."

The players wanted to give me some nickname other than "Kid." Someone suggested

"Ducky" in honor of my running style. "Fats" said somebody else. I made a note to remove his bookmark between innings. Several other suggestions were downright obscene. Baseball players, in spite of their obsession with literature and the arts, often have a bawdy sense of humor.

"How about 'Moonlight,'" I suggested. I'd read about an old-time player who stopped for a cup of coffee with the Giants half a century before, who had that nickname.

"What the hell for?" said Monty Irvin, who in spite of the nickname preferred to be called Monford or even by his second name, Merrill. "You got to have a reason for a nickname. You got to earn it. Still, anything is better than W. P."

"It was only a suggestion," I said. I made a mental note to tell Monford what I knew about *his* favorite author, Erskine Caldwell.

As it turned out I didn't earn a nickname until the day we won the pennant.

As every baseball fan knows, the Giants went into the bottom of the ninth in the deciding game of the pennant playoff trailing the Dodgers 4-1.

"Don't worry," I said to Durocher, "everything's going to work out." If he heard me he didn't let on.

But was everything going to work out? And what part was I going to play in it? Even though I'd contributed to the Giants' amazing stretch drive, I didn't belong. Why am I here? I kept asking myself. I had some vague premonition that I was about to change history. I mean I wasn't a ballplayer. I was a writer. Here I was about to go into Grade 12 and I was already planning to do my master's thesis on F. Scott Fitzgerald.

I didn't have time to worry further as Alvin Dark singled. Don Mueller, in his

14

excitement, had carried his copy of *The Mill on the Floss* out to the on-deck circle. He set the resin bag on top of it, stalked to the plate and singled, moving Dark to second.

I was flabbergasted when Durocher called Monford Irvin back and said to me "Get in there, Kid."

It was at that moment that I knew why I was there. I would indeed change history. One stroke of the bat and the score would be tied. I eyed the left-field stands as I nervously swung two bats to warm up. I was nervous but not scared. I never doubted my prowess for one moment. Years later Johnny Bench summed it up for both athletes and writers when he talked about a successful person having to have an *inner conceit*. It never occurred to me until days later that I might have hit into a double or triple play, thus ending it and *really* changing history.

When I did take my place in the batter's box, I pounded the plate and glared out at Don Newcombe. I wished that I shaved so I could give him a stubble-faced stare of contempt. He curved me and I let it go by for a ball. I fouled the next pitch high into the first-base stands. A fastball was low. I fouled the next one outside third. I knew he didn't want to go to a full count: I crowded the plate a little looking for the fastball. He curved me. Nervy. But the curveball hung, sat out over the plate like a cantaloupe. I waited an extra millisecond before lambasting it. In that instant that ball broke in on my hands; it hit the bat right next to my right hand. It has been over thirty years but I still wake deep in the night, my hands vibrating, burning from Newcombe's pitch. The bat shattered into kindling. The ball flew in a polite loop as if it had been tossed by a five-year-old; it landed soft as a creampuff in Peewee Reese's glove. One out.

I slumped back to the bench.

15

"Tough luck, Kid," said Durocher, patting my shoulder. "There'll be other chances to be a hero."

"Thanks, Leo," I said.

Whitey Lockman doubled. Dark scored. Mueller hurt himself sliding into third. Rafael Noble went in to run for Mueller. Charlie Dressen replaced Newcombe with Ralph Branca. Bobby Thomson swung bats in the on-deck circle.

As soon as the umpire Jorda called time-in, Durocher leapt to his feet, and before Bobby Thomson could take one step toward the plate, Durocher called him back.

"Don't do that!" I yelled, suddenly knowing why I was *really* there. But Durocher ignored me. He was beckoning with a big-knuckled finger to another reserve player, a big outfielder who was tearing up the American Association when they brought him up late in the year. He was 5 for 8 as a pinch hitter.

Durocher was already up the dugout steps heading toward the umpire to announce the change. The outfielder from the American Association was making his way down the dugout, hopping along over feet and ankles. He'd be at the top of the step by the time Durocher reached the umpire.

As he skipped by me, the last person between Bobby Thomson and immortality, I stuck out my foot. The outfielder from the American Association went down like he'd been poleaxed. He hit his face on the top step of the dugout, crying out loud enough to attract Durocher's attention.

The trainer hustled the damaged player to the clubhouse. Durocher waved Bobby Thomson to the batter's box. And the rest is history. After the victory celebration I announced my retirement, blaming it on a damaged wrist. I went back to Iowa and listened

16

to the World Series on the radio.

All I have to show that I ever played in the major leagues is my one-line entry in *The Baseball Encyclopedia*:

W. P. KINSELLA Kinsella, William Patrick "Tripper" BR TR 5'9"
    185 lbs. B. Apr. 14, 1934 Onamata, Ia.

Pinch Hit 1951 NY N

G 38 AB 33 H 11 2B 2 3B 0 HR 2 HR% 6.0 R 0 RBI 8

BB 4 SO 4 EA 0 BA .333 AB 33 H 11

I got my outright release in the mail the week after the World Series ended. Durocher had scrawled across the bottom: "Good luck, Kid. By the way, *The Great Gatsby* is *not* an allegory."

you could look it up

It all begun when we dropped down to C'lumbus, Ohio, from Pittsburgh to play a exhibition game on our way out to St. Louis. It was gettin' on into September, and though we'd been leadin' the league by six, seven games most of the season, we was now in first place by a margin you could'a' got it into the eye of a thimble, bein' only a half a game ahead of St. Louis. Our slump had given the boys the leapin' jumps, and they was like a bunch of old ladies at a lawn fete with a thunderstorm comin' up, runnin' around snarlin' at each other, eatin' bad and sleepin' worse, and battin' for a team average of maybe .186. Half the time nobody'd speak to nobody else, without it was to bawl 'em out.

Squawks Magrew was managin' the boys at the time, and he was darn near crazy. They called him "Squawks" 'cause when things was goin' bad, he lost his voice, or perty near

james thurber

lost it, and squealed at you like a little girl you stepped on her doll or somethin'. He yelled at everybody and wouldn't listen to nobody, without maybe it was me. I'd been trainin' the boys for ten year, and he'd take more lip from me than from anybody else. He knowed I was smarter'n him, anyways, like you're goin' to hear.

This was thirty, thirty-one year ago; you could look it up, 'cause it was the same year C'lumbus decided to call itself the Arch City, on account of a lot of iron arches with electric-light bulbs into 'em which stretched acrost High Street. Thomas Albert Edison sent 'em a telegram, and they was speeches and maybe even President Taft opened the celebration by pushin' a button. It was a great week for the Buckeye capital, which was why they got us out there for this exhibition game.

Well, we just lose a double-header to Pittsburgh, 11 to 5 and 7 to 3, so we snarled all the way to C'lumbus, where we put up at the Chittaden Hotel, still snarlin'. Everybody was tetchy, and when Billy Klinger took a sock at Whitey Cott at breakfast, Whitey throwed marmalade all over his face.

"Blind each other, watta I care?" says Magrew. "You can't see nothin' anyways."

C'lumbus win the exhibition game, 3 to 2, whilst Magrew set in the dugout, mutterin' and cursin' like a fourteen-year-old Scotty. He bad-mouthed everybody on the ball club and he bad-mouthed everybody offa the ball club, includin' the Wright brothers, who, he claimed, had yet to build a airship big enough for any of our boys to hit with a ball bat.

"I wisht I was dead," he says to me. "I wisht I was in heaven with the angels."

I told him to pull hisself together, 'cause he was drivin' the boys crazy, the way he was goin' on and sulkin' and bad-mouthin' and whinin'. I was older'n he was and smarter'n he was, and he knowed it. I was ten times smarter'n he was about this Pearl

du Monville, first time I ever laid eyes on the little guy, which was one of the saddest days of my life.

Now, most people name of Pearl is girls, but this Pearl du Monville was a man, if you could call a fella a man who was only thirty-four, thirty-five inches high. Pearl du Monville was a midget. He was part French and part Hungarian, and maybe even part Bulgarian or somethin'. I can see him now, a sneer on his little pushed-in pan, swingin' a bamboo cane and smokin' a big cigar. He had a gray suit with a big black check into it, and he had a gray felt hat with one of them rainbow-colored hatbands onto it, like the young fellas wore in them days. He talked like he was talkin' into a tin can, but he didn't have no foreign accent. He might a been fifteen or he might a been a hundred, you couldn't tell. Pearl du Monville.

After the game with C'lumbus, Magrew headed straight for the Chittaden bar — the train for St. Louis wasn't goin' for three, four hours — and there he set, drinkin' rye and talkin' to this bartender.

"How I pity me, brother," Magrew was tellin' this bartender. "How I pity me." That was alwuz his favorite tune. So he was settin' there, tellin' this bartender how heart-breakin' it was to be manager of a bunch a blindfolded circus clowns, when up pops this Pearl du Monville outa nowheres.

It give Magrew the leapin' jumps. He thought at first maybe the D.T.'s had come back on him; he claimed he'd had 'em once, and little guys had popped up all around him, wearin' red, white, and blue hats.

"Go on, now!" Magrew yells. "Get away from me!"

But the midget clumb up on a chair acrost the table from Magrew and says, "I seen that game today, Junior, and you ain't got no ball club. What you got there, Junior," he says, "is a side show."

"Whatta ya mean, 'Junior'?" says Magrew, touchin' the little guy to satisfy hisself he was real.

"Don't pay him no attention, mister," says the bartender. "Pearl calls everybody 'Junior,' 'cause it always turns out he's a year older'n anybody else."

"Yeh?" says Magrew. "How old is he?"

"How old are you, Junior?" says the midget.

"Who, me? I'm fifty-three," says Magrew.

"Well, I'm fifty-four," says the midget.

Magrew grins and asts him what he'll have, and that was the beginnin' of their beautiful friendship, if you don't care what you say.

Pearl du Monville stood up on his chair and waved his cane around and pretended like he was ballyhooin' for a circus. "Right this way, folks!" he yells. "Come on in and see the greatest collection of freaks in the world! See the armless pitchers, see the eyeless batters, see the infielders with five thumbs!" and on like that, feedin' Magrew gall and handin' him a laugh at the same time, you might say.

You could hear him and Pearl du Monville hootin' and hollerin' and singin' way up to the fourth floor of the Chittaden, where the boys was packin' up. When it come time to got to the station, you can imagine how disgusted we was when we crowded into the doorway of that bar and seen them two singin' and goin' on.

"Well, well, well," says Magrew, lookin' up and spottin' us. "Look who's here . . . . Clowns, this is Pearl du Monville, a monseer of the old, old school . . . . Don't shake

23

hands with 'em, Pearl, 'cause their fingers is made of chalk and would bust right off in your paws," he says, and he starts guffawin' and Pearl starts titterin' and we stand there givin' 'em the iron eye, it bein' the lowest ebb a ball-club manager'd got hisself down to since the national pastime was started.

Then the midget begun givin' us the ballyhoo. "Come on in!" he says, wavin' his cane. "See the legless base runners, see the outfielders with the butter fingers, see the southpaw with the arm of a little chee-ild!"

Then him and Magrew begun to hoop and holler and nudge each other till you'd of thought this little guy was the funniest guy than even Charlie Chaplin. The fellas filed outa the bar without a word and went on up to the Union Depot, leavin' me to handle Magrew and his new-found crony.

Well, I got 'em outa there finely. I had to take the little guy along, 'cause Magrew had a holt onto him like a vise and I couldn't pry him loose.

"He's comin' along as masket," says Magrew, holdin' the midget in the crouch of his arm like a football. And come along he did, hollerin' and protestin' and beatin' at Magrew with his little fists.

"Cut it out, will ya, Junior?" the little guy kept whinin'. "Come on, leave a man loose, will ya, Junior?"

But Junior kept a holt onto him and begun yellin', "See the guys with the cast-iron brains, see the fielders with the feet on their wrists!"

So it goes, right through the whole Union Depot, with people starin' and catcallin', and he don't put the midget down till he gets him through the gates.

"How'm I goin' to go along without no toothbrush?" the midget asts. "What'm I goin'

24

to do without no other suit?" he says.

"Doc here," says Magrew, meanin' me — "doc here will look after you like you was his own son, won't you, doc?"

I give him the iron eye, and he finely got on the train and prob'ly went to sleep with his clothes on.

This left me alone with the midget. "Lookit," I says to him. "Why don't you go on home now? Come mornin', Magrew'll forget all about you. He'll prob'ly think you was somethin' he seen in a nightmare maybe. And he ain't goin' to laugh so easy in the mornin', neither," I says. "So why don't you go on home?"

"Nix," he says to me. "Skiddoo," he says, "twenty-three for you," and he tosses his cane up into the vestibule of the coach and clam'ers on up after it like a cat. So that's the way Pearl du Monville come to go to St. Louis with the ball club.

I seen 'em first at breakfast the next day, settin' opposite each other; the midget playin' "Turkey in the Straw" on a harmonium and Magrew starin' at his eggs and bacon like they was a uncooked bird with its feathers still on.

"Remember where you found this?" I says, jerkin' my thumb at the midget. "Or maybe you think they come with breakfast on these trains," I says, bein' a good hand at turnin' a sharp remark in them days.

The midget puts down the harmonium and turns on me. "Sneeze," he says; "your brains is dusty." Then he snaps a couple drops of water at me from a tumbler. "Drown," he says, tryin' to make his voice deep.

Now, both them cracks is Civil War cracks, but you'd of thought they was brand-new and the funniest than any crack Magrew'd ever heard in his whole life. He started hoopin'

25

and hollerin', so I walked on away and set down with Bugs Courtney and Hank Metters, payin' no attention to this weak-minded Damon and Phidias acrost the aisle.

Well, sir, the first game with St. Louis was rained out, and there we was facin' a double-header next day. Like maybe I told you, we lose the last three double-headers we play, makin' maybe twenty-five errors in the six games, which is all right for the intimates of a school for the blind, but is disgraceful for the world's champions. It was too wet to go to the zoo, and Magrew wouldn't let us go to the movies, 'cause they flickered so bad in them days. So we just set around, stewin' and frettin'.

One of the newspaper boys come over to take a pitture of Billy Klinger and Whitey Cott shakin' hands — this reporter'd heard about the fight — and whilst they was standin' there, toe to toe, shakin' hands, Billy give a back lunge and a jerk, and throwed Whitey over his shoulder into a corner of the room, like a sack a salt. Whitey come back at him with a chair, and Bethlehem broke loose in that there room. The camera was tromped to pieces like a berry basket. When we finely got 'em pulled apart, I heard a laugh, and there was Magrew and the midget standin' in the door and givin' us the iron eye.

"Wrasslers," says Magrew, coldlike, "that's what I got for a ball club, Mr. Du Monville, wrasslers — and not very good wrasslers at that, you ast me."

"A man can't be good at everythin'," says Pearl, "but he oughta be good at somethin'."

This sets Magrew guffawin' again, and away they go, the midget taggin' along by his side like a hound dog and handin' him a fast line of so-called comic cracks.

When we went out to face that battlin' St. Louis club in a double-header the next afternoon, the boys was jumpy as tin toys with keys in their back. We lose the first game, 7 to 2, and are trailin', 4 to 0, when the second game ain't but ten minutes old. Magrew set

26

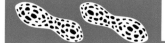

there like a stone statue, speakin' to nobody. Then, in their half a the fourth, somebody singled to center and knocked in two more runs for St. Louis.

That made Magrew squawk. "I wisht one thing," he says. "I wisht I was manager of a old ladies' sewin' circus 'stead of a ball club."

"You are, Junior, you are," says a familyer and disagreeable voice.

It was that Pearl du Monville again, poppin' up out of nowheres, swingin' his bamboo cane and smokin' a cigar that's three sizes too big for his face. By this time we'd finely got the other side out, and Hank Metters slithered a bat acrost the ground, and the midget had to jump to keep both his ankles from bein' broke.

I thought Magrew'd bust a blood vessel. "You hurt Pearl and I'll break your neck!" he yelled.

Hank muttered somethin' and went on up to the plate and struck out.

We managed to get a couple runs acrost in our half a the sixth, but they come back with three more in their half a the seventh, and this was too much for Magrew.

"Come on, Pearl," he says. "We're gettin' outa here."

"Where you think you're goin'?" I ast him.

"To the lawyer's again," he says cryptly.

"I didn't know you'd been to the lawyer's once, yet," I says.

"Which that goes to show how much you don't know," he says.

28

With that, they was gone, and I didn't see 'em the rest of the day, nor know what they was up to, which was a God's blessin'. We lose the nightcap, 9 to 3, and that puts us into second place plenty, and as low in our mind as a ball club can get.

The next day was a horrible day, like anybody that lived through it can tell you.

 **thurber**

Practice was just over and the St. Louis club was takin' the field, when I hears this strange sound from the stands. It sounds like the nervous whickerin' a horse gives when he smells somethin' funny on the wind. It was the fans ketchin' sight of Pearl du Monville, like you have prob'ly guessed. The midget had popped up onto the field all dressed up in a minacher club uniform, sox, cap, little letters sewed onto his chest, and all. He was swingin' a kid's bat and the only thing kept him from lookin' like a real ballplayer seen through the wrong end of a microscope was this cigar he was smokin'.

Bugs Courtney reached over and jerked it outa his mouth and throwed it away. "You're wearin' that suit on the playin' field," he says to him, severe as a judge. "You go insultin' it and I'll take you out to the zoo and feed you to the bears."

Pearl just blowed some smoke at him which he still has in his mouth.

Whilst Whitey was foulin' off four or five prior to strikin' out, I went on over to Magrew. "If I was as comic as you," I says, "I'd laugh myself to death," I says. "Is that any way to treat the uniform, makin' a mockery out of it?"

"It might surprise you to know I ain't makin' no mockery outa the uniform," says Magrew. "Pearl du Monville here has been made a bone-of-fida member of this so-called ball club. I fixed it up with the front office by long-distance phone."

"Yeah?" I says. "I can just hear Mr. Dillworth or Bart Jenkins agreein' to hire a midget for the ball club. I can just hear 'em." Mr. Dillworth was the owner of the club and Bart Jenkins was the secretary, and they never stood for no monkey business. "May I be so bold as to inquire," I says, "just what you told 'em?"

"I told 'em," he says, "I wanted to sign up a guy they ain't no pitcher in the league can strike him out."

29

"Uh-huh," I says, "and did you tell 'em what size of a man he is?"

"Never mind about that," he says. "I got papers on me, made out legal and proper, con-stitutin' one Pearl du Monville a bone-of-fida member of this former ball club. Maybe that'll shame them big babies into gettin' in there and swingin', knowin' I can replace any one of 'em with a midget, if I have a mind to. A St. Louis lawyer I seen twice tells me it's all legal and proper."

"A St. Louis lawyer would," I says, "seein' nothin' could make him happier than havin' you makin' a mockery outa this one-time baseball outfit," I says.

Well, sir, it'll all be there in the papers of thirty, thirty-one year ago, and you could look it up. The game went along with no scorin' for seven innings, and since they ain't nothin' much to watch but guys poppin' up or strikin' out, the fans pay most of their attention on the goin's-on of Pearl du Monville. He's out there in front a the dugout, turnin' hand-springs, balancin' his hat on his chin, walkin' a imaginary line, and so on. The fans clapped and laughed at him, and he ate it up.

So it went up to the last a the eighth, nothin' to nothin', not more'n seven, eight hits all told, and no errors on neither side. Our pitcher gets the first two men out easy in the eighth. Then up come a fella name of Porter or Billings, or some such name, and he lammed one up against the tobacco sign for three bases. The next guy up slapped the first ball out into left for a base hit, and in come the fella from third for the only run of the game so far. The crowd yelled, the look a death come onto Magrew's face again, and even the midget quit his tomfoolin'. Their next man fouled out back a third, and we come up for our last bats like a bunch a schoolgirls steppin' into a pool of cold water. I was lower in my mind than I'd been since the day in nineteen-four when Chesbro throwed the wild

30

pitch in the ninth inning with a man on third and lost the pennant for the Highlanders. I knowed somethin' just as bad was goin' to happen, which shows I'm a clairvoyun, or was then.

When Gordy Mills hit out to second, I just closed my eyes. I opened 'em up again to see Dutch Miller standin' on second, dustin' off his pants, him havin' got his first hit in maybe twenty times to the plate. Next up was Harry Loesing, battin' for our pitcher, and he got a base on balls, walkin' on a fourth one you could a combed your hair with.

Then up come Whitey Cott, our lead-off man. He crouches down in what was prob'ly the most fearsome stanch in organized ball, but all he can do is pop out to short. That brung up Billy Klinger, with two down and a man on first and second. Billy took a cut at one you could a knocked a plug hat offa this here Carnera with it, but then he gets sense enough to wait 'em out, and finely he walks, too, fillin' the bases.

Yes, sir, there you are; the tyin' run on third and the winnin' run on second, first a the ninth, two men down, and Hank Metters comin' to the bat. Hank was built like a Pope-Hartford and he couldn't run no faster'n President Taft, but he had five homeruns to his credit for the season, and that wasn't bad in them days. Hank was still hittin' better'n anybody else on the ball club, and it was mighty heartenin', seein' him stridin' up towards the plate. But he never got there.

"Wait a minute!" yells Magrew, jumpin' to his feet. "I'm sendin' in a pinch hitter!" he yells.

You could a heard a bomb drop. When a ball club manager says he's sendin' in a pinch hitter for the best batter on the club, you know and I know and everybody knows he's lost his holt.

thurber

"They're goin' to be sendin' the funny wagon for you, if you don't watch out," I says, grabbin' a holt of his arm.

But he pulled away and run out towards the plate, yellin', "Du Monville battin' for Metters!"

All the fellas begun squawlin' at once, except Hank, and he just stood there starin' at Magrew like he'd gone crazy and was claimin' to be Ty Cobb's grandma or somethin'. Their pitcher stood out there with his hands on his hips and a disagreeable look on his face, and the plate umpire told Magrew to go on and get a batter up. Magrew told him again du Monville was battin' for Metters, and the St. Louis manager finely got the idea. It brung him outa his dugout howlin' and bawlin' like he'd lost a female dog and her seven pups.

Magrew pushed the midget towards the plate and he says to him, he says, "Just stand up there and hold that bat on your shoulder. They ain't a man in the world can throw three strikes in there 'fore he throws four balls!" he says.

"I get it, Junior!" says the midget. "He'll walk me and force in the tyin' run!" And he starts on up to the plate as cocky as if he was Willie Keeler.

I don't need to tell you Bethlehem broke loose on that there ball field. The fans got onto their hind legs, yellin' and whistlin', and everybody on the field begun wavin' their arms and hollerin' and shovin'. The plate umpire stalked over to Magrew like a traffic cop, waggin' his jaw and pointin' his finger, and the St. Louis manager kept yellin' like his house was on fire. When Pearl got up to the plate and stood there, the pitcher slammed his glove down onto the ground and started stompin' on it, and they ain't nobody can blame him. He's just walked two normal-sized human bein's, and now here's a guy up to the plate they ain't more'n twenty inches between his knees and his shoulders.

The plate umpire called in the field umpire, and they talked a while, like a couple doctors seein' the bucolic plague or somethin' for the first time. Then the plate umpire come over to Magrew with his arms folded acrost his chest, and he told him to go and get a batter up, or he'd forfeit the game to St. Louis. He pulled out his watch, but somebody batted it outa his hand in the scufflin', and I thought there'd be a free-for-all, with everybody yellin' and shovin' except Pearl du Monville, who stood up at the plate with his little bat on his shoulder, not movin' a muscle.

Then Magrew played his ace. I seen him pull some papers outa his pocket and show 'em to the plate umpire. The umpire began lookin' at 'em like they was bills for somethin' he not only never bought it, he never even heard of it. The other umpire studied 'em like they was a death warren, and all the time the St. Louis manager and the fans and the players is yellin' and hollerin'.

Well, sir, they fought about him bein' a midget, and they fought about him usin' a kid's bat, and they fought about where he'd been all season. They was eight or nine rule books brung out and everybody was thumbin' through 'em tryin' to find out what it says about midgets, 'cause this was somethin' never'd come up in the history of the game before, and nobody'd ever dreamed about it, even when they has nightmares. Maybe you can't send no midgets in to bat nowadays, 'cause the old game's changed a lot, mostly for the worst, but you could then, it turned out.

The plate umpire finely decided the contrack papers was all legal and proper, like Magrew said, so he waved the St. Louis players back to their places and he pointed his finger at their manager and told him to quit hollerin' and get on back in the dugout. The manager says the game is percedin' under protest, and the umpire bawls, "Play ball!" over 'n' above the yellin' and booin', him havin' a voice like a hog caller.

The St. Louis pitcher picked up his glove and beat it with his fist six or eight times, and then got set on the mound and studied the situation. The fans realized he was really goin' to pitch to the midget, and they went crazy, hoopin' and hollerin' louder'n ever, and throwin' pop bottles and hats and cushions down onto the field. It took five, ten minutes to get the fans quieted down again, whilst our fellas that was on base set down on the bags and waited. And Pearl du Monville kept standin' up there with the bat on his shoulder, like he'd been told to.

So the pitcher starts studyin' the setup again, and you got to admit it was the strangest setup in a ball game since the players cut off their beards and begun wearin' gloves. I wisht I could call the pitcher's name — it wasn't old Barney Pelty nor Jack Powell nor Harry Howell. He was a big right-hander, but I can't call his name. You could look it up. Even in a crotchin' position, the ketcher towers over the midget like the Washington Monument.

The plate umpire tries standin' on his tiptoes, then he tries crotchin' down, and he finely gets hisself into a stanch nobody'd ever seen on a ball field before, kinda squattin' down on his hanches.

Well, the pitcher is sore as a old buggy horse in fly time. He slams in the first pitch, hard and wild, and maybe two foot higher'n the midget's head.

"Ball one!" hollers the umpire over 'n' above the racket, 'cause everybody is yellin' worsten ever.

The ketcher goes out towards the mound and talks to the pitcher and hands him the ball. This time the big right-hander tried a undershoot, and it comes in a little closer,

35

maybe no higher'n a foot, foot and a half above Pearl's head. It would a been a strike with a human bein' in there, but the umpire's got to call it, and he does.

"Ball two!" he bellers.

The ketcher walks out to the mound again, and the whole infield comes over and gives advice to the pitcher about what they'd do in a case like this, with two balls and no strikes on a batter that oughta be in a bottle of alcohol 'stead of up there at the plate in a big-league game between the teams that is fightin' for first place.

For the third pitch, the pitcher stands there flat-footed and tosses up the ball like he's playin' ketch with a little girl.

Pearl stands there motionless as a hitchin' post, and the ball comes in big and slow and high — high for Pearl, that is, it bein' about on a level with his eyes, or a little higher'n a grown man's knees.

They ain't nothin' else for the umpire to do, so he calls, "Ball three!"

Everybody is onto their feet, hoopin' and hollerin', as the pitcher sets to throw ball four. The St. Louis manager is makin' signs and faces like he was a contorturer, and the infield is givin' the pitcher some more advice about what to do this time. Our boys who was on base stick right onto the bag, runnin' no risk of bein' nipped for the last out.

Well, the pitcher decides to give him a toss again, seein' he come closer with that than a fast ball. They ain't nobody ever seen a slower ball throwed. It come in big as a balloon and slower'n any ball ever throwed before in the major leagues. It come right in over the plate in front of Pearl's chest, lookin' prob'ly big as a full moon to Pearl. They ain't never been a minute like the minute that followed since the United States was founded by the Pilgrim grandfathers.

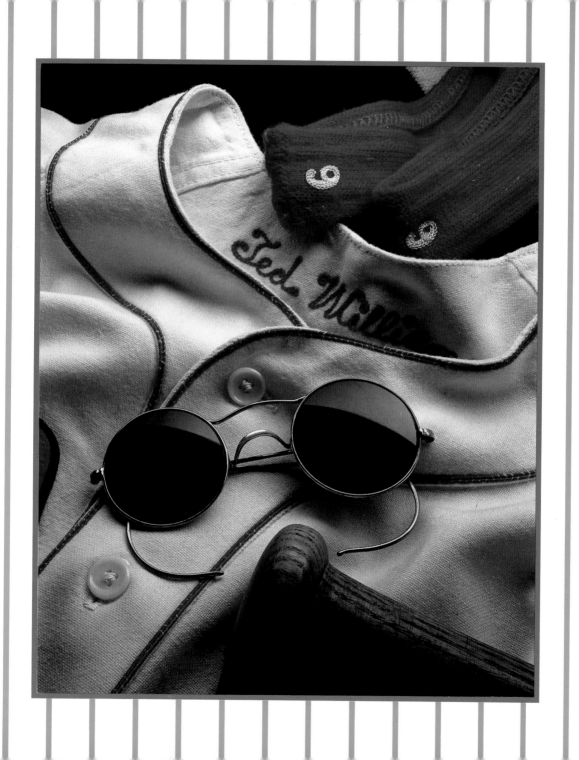

Pearl du Monville took a cut at that ball, and he hit it! Magrew give a groan like a poleaxed steer as the ball rolls out in front a the plate into fair territory.

"Fair ball!" yells the umpire, and the midget starts runnin' for first, still carryin' that little bat, and makin' maybe ninety foot an hour. Bethlehem breaks loose on that ball field and in them stands. They ain't been nothin' like it since creation was begun.

The ball's rollin' slow, on down towards third, goin' maybe eight, ten foot. The infield comes in fast and our boys break from their bases like hares in a brush fire. Everybody is standin' up, yellin' and hollerin', and Magrew is tearin' his hair outa his head, and the midget is scamperin' for first with all the speed of one of them little dashhounds carryin' a satchel in his mouth.

The ketcher gets to the ball first, but he boots it on out past the pitcher's box, the pitcher fallin' on his face tryin' to stop it, the shortstop sprawlin' after it full length and zaggin' it on over towards the second baseman, whilst Muller is scorin' with the tyin' run and Loesing is roundin' third with the winnin' run. Ty Cobb could a made a three-bagger outa that bunt, with everybody fallin' over theirself tryin' to pick the ball up. But Pearl is still maybe fifteen, twenty feet from the bag, toddlin' like a baby and yeepin' like a trapped rabbit, when the second baseman finely gets a holt of that ball and slams it over to first. The first baseman ketches it and stomps on the bag, the base umpire waves Pearl out, and there goes your old ball game, the craziest ball game ever played in the history of the organized world.

Their players start runnin' in, and then I see Magrew. He starts after Pearl, runnin' faster'n any man ever run before. Pearl sees him comin' and runs behind the base umpire's legs and gets a holt onto 'em. Magrew comes up, pantin' and roarin', and him

38

and the midget plays ring-around-a-rosy with the umpire, who keeps shovin' at Magrew with one hand and tryin' to slap the midget loose from his legs with the other.

Finely Magrew ketches the midget, who is still yeepin' like a stuck sheep. He gets holt of that little guy by both his ankles and starts whirlin' him round and round his head like Magrew was a hammer thrower and Pearl was the hammer. Nobody can stop him without gettin' their head knocked off, so everybody just stands there and yells. Then Magrew lets the midget fly. He flies on out towards second, high and fast, like a human homerun, headed for the soap sign in center field.

Their shortstop tries to get him, but he can't make it, and I knowed the little fella was goin' to bust to pieces like a dollar watch on a asphalt street when he hit the ground. But it so happens their center fielder is just crossin' second, and he starts runnin' back, tryin' to get under the midget, who had took to spiralin' like a football 'stead of turnin' head over foot, which give him more speed and more distance.

I know you never seen a midget ketched, and you probably never seen one throwed. To ketch a midget that's been throwed by a heavy-muscled man and is flyin' through the air, you got to run under him and with him and pull your hands and arms back and down when you ketch him, to break the compact of his body, or you'll bust him in two like a match-stick. I seen Bill Lange and Willie Keeler and Tris Speaker make some wonderful ketches in my day, but I never seen nothin' like that center fielder. He goes back and back and still further back and he pulls that midget down outa the air like he was liftin' a sleepin' baby from a cradle. There wasn't a bruise onto him, only his face was the color of cat's meat and he ain't got no air in his chest. In his excitement, the base umpire, who was runnin' back with the center fielder when he ketched Pearl, yells, "Out!" and that give hysteries to

39

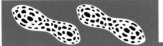

the Bethlehem which was ragin' like Niagry on that ball field.

Everybody was hoopin' and hollerin' and yellin' and runnin', and the fans swarmin' onto the field, and the cops tryin' to keep order, and some guys laughin' and some women fans cryin', and six or eight of us holdin' onto Magrew to keep him from gettin' at that midget and finishin' him off. Some of the fans picks up the St. Louis pitcher and the center fielder and starts carryin' 'em around on their shoulders, and they was the craziest goin's-on knowed to the history of organized ball on this side of the 'Lantic Ocean.

I seen Pearl du Monville strugglin' in the arms of a lady fan with a ample bossom, who was laughin' and cryin' at the same time, and him beatin' at her with his little fists and bawlin' and yellin'. He clawed his way loose finely and disappeared in the forest of legs which made that ball field look like it was Coney Island on a hot summer's day.

That was the last I ever seen of Pearl du Monville. I never seen hide nor hair of him from that day to this, and neither did nobody else. He just vanished into the thin of the air, as the fella says. He was ketched for the final out of the ball game and that was the end of him, just like it was the end of the ball game, you might say, and also the end of our losin' streak, like I'm goin' to tell you.

That night we piled onto a train for Chicago, but we wasn' snarlin' and snappin' any more. No, sir, the ice was finely broke and a new spirit come into that ball club. The old zip come back with the disappearance of Pearl du Monville out back a second base. We got to laughin' and talkin' and kiddin' together, and 'fore long Magrew was laughin' with us. He got a human look onto his pan again, and he quit whinin' and complainin' and wishtin' he was in heaven with the angels.

Well, sir, we wiped up that Chicago series, winnin' all four games, and makin'

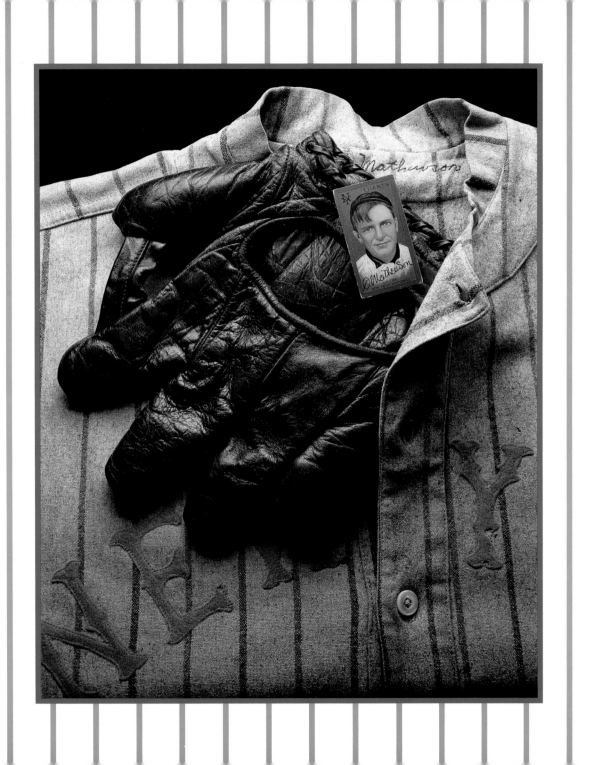

seventeen hits in one of 'em. Funny thing was, St. Louis was so shook up by that last game with us, they never did hit their stride again. Their center fielder took to misjudgin' everythin' that come his way, and the rest a the fellas followed suit, the way a club'll do when one guy blows up.

'Fore we left Chicago, I and some fellas went out and bought a pair of them little baby shoes, which we had 'em golded over and give 'em to Magrew for a souvenir, and he took it all in good spirit. Whitey Cott and Billy Klinger made up and was fast friends again, and we hit our home lot like a ton of dynamite and they was nothin' could stop us from then on.

I don't recollect things as clear as I did thirty, forty years ago. I can't read no fine print no more, and the only person I got to check with on the golden days of the national pastime, as the fella says, is my friend, old Milt Kline, over in Springfield, and his mind ain't as strong as it once was.

He gets Rube Waddell mixed up with Rube Marquard, for one thing, and anybody does that oughta be put away where he won't bother nobody. So I can't tell you the exact margin we win the pennant by. Maybe it was two and a half games, or maybe it was three and a half. But it'll all be there in the newspapers and record books of thirty, thirty-one year ago and, like I was sayin', you could look it up.

42

the rollicking god

Here and now, before the high bar of public opinion, I charge Marshall Mount of the New York *Sphere* and Smack Riley of the Grays with having cost the Grays the pennant last year.

You know Mount, of course. You've been pestered undoubtedly with quotations from his column, "In My Humble Opinion," which appears on the *Sphere*'s sporting page each morning.

"Did you see what Marshall Mount said about Benny Leonard — how he said Benny is the Saint-Saëns of the ring?" Or, as likely as not, you quote him yourself. "What do you think of Marshall Mount's calling Hank Gowdy the Schopenhauer of the diamond?" Stuff like that.

And as for Smack, who doesn't know him and his big bat?

These, then, are the facts, the evidence: It was in April, during the first home

nunnally johnson

johnson

series at the stadium, that I met Mount, a tall, lanky, frowzy young fellow, shambling a little and with no taste whatever in neckties. He slid into a working-press seat at my side. At first, never having seen him before, I took him to be just another actor, one with more nerve than usual. He had a kind of embarrassed air, and as he sat down he dropped a couple of new books which, I suppose, he'd brought along to read during the more exciting parts of the game. When he leaned over to pick them up he dropped three pencils out of his pocket, and while picking up the pencils he dropped a notebook, three letters, a pocket comb, two mothballs and a baby's nursing bottle. He was that kind of bird.

"You ought to tie all those things to you with strings," I said, "or else carry a postman's satchel."

"I don't know," he replied doubtfully, weighing the suggestions. "They never dropped out before. At least, not so many of them at once. Have you got a cigarette?"

There's no man living can call me a tightwad, so I gave him one. Then it occurred to me, after witnessing his search through every pocket and the nursing bottle, that he needed a match. He thanked me, lit the cigarette and produced a score book.

The game that day was, as I said next morning in the *Ledger,* a wow. It seesawed for a while, and then in the end good old Smack Riley ambled up to the pan, leaned on one of Coveleskie's fast ones, and sweet COOKIE! — into the Harlem River, or nearly. It was the Smacker's first homer of the season at the Stadium.

I've learned pretty well to control myself in crises like this, for if we baseball writers aren't calm, who will be? But this fellow on my left, this Mount, sprang to his feet, spilling his books, his pencils and three new and theretofore undiscovered mothballs, and let out a roar:

"Beautiful!"

44

johnson

Honestly, I just looked at him.

"What did you say?" I asked.

"I say he's beautiful, positively beautiful!"

"If you mean Smack" — and any man in the *Ledger* office will tell you if I can be sarcastic or not — "then you ought to wait and see Nick Altrock."

He looked actually impatient — and me the dean of sporting writers!

"His swing," he explained; "the way he threw his body into that terrific effort. It was just a flash, the fraction of a second of it; but it was rhythm, grace, beauty. It reminded me, truly, of Walter Pater — just for that instant."

As my friends will tell you, I am a plain man, a baseball reporter with no frills. What this bird was talking about I did not know. Smack had hit a homerun. The game belonged to the Grays. What else was going on, I, speaking personally, could not see.

"Beautiful!" he repeated. "I never had any idea that a baseball player could crystallize so much of authentic glory in one movement."

"What are you, anyway," I demanded — "one of these poets?"

"Oh, excuse me," he replied hastily — we were getting our stuff together to climb out. "My name is Mount. I'm from the *Sphere*. I'm going to cover the Grays for a while." Then he added, as though to himself, "All season, I hope. I'd like to see that fellow again. It was marvelous, that swing."

"Well," I said amiably, for after all he was one of us baseball reporters, "as long as they don't come three at a time it's jake with me."

As he climbed up the stairs to the runway his left garter broke and dragged on the ground behind him.

johnson

I may as well add right here that as the season went along I found out that that fellow found all that beauty he was talking about in strikes as well as homeruns. One day I remember he wrote:

"There is a strength in one of Riley's swings, even when he misses the ball, that holds all the coordination of which the human body is capable. In this ball player's mighty failures there is a lesson for our young playwrights, a lesson that Eugene O'Neill had already learned. We believe that we had rather see Smack Riley strike out than any other player make a hit. Life is not so much what one gains as what one tries for."

Right then and there he ought to have been hanged.

The next morning after that meeting I looked up his story. Well, I clipped it out. I was going to save it for the Smithsonian Institution. It was what one might easily call a jewel. What he had said at the Stadium about Smack Riley's beauty was just a suggestion of what he had to say in his story about it. Grace, ease, coordinated effort, rhythm, beauty — all that was in a baseball story. Furthermore, in that same story there were two mentions of George Bernard Shaw, one each of Rudolph Valentino, Lord Dunsany, Man o' War, Professor Copeland of Harvard, and seven of Eugene O'Neill. He included also three actresses, two books and five plays. The only way you could tell it was a baseball story was the box score at the end; and, honestly, when I looked I half expected to find a cast of characters. As I said, I was going to save it, but a week later I threw it away. All his stories turned out to be like that.

That afternoon I went to Harry Kelly of the *Blade*.

"Who is this Mount?" I said. "And what theater does he think today's game is being played in?"

johnson

Harry wasn't sure. Mount had come from Rutgers, he said, had lived south of Washington Square and had written two one-act plays, the kind that are produced by companies that are just a lot of aesthetes together, giving everything for art, gratis. He'd been on the *Sphere* two years. First he was rewriting, but they'd had to take him off that. Every story he wrote, whether it was about a five-legged calf in Lima, Ohio, or a fire on the Brooklyn waterfront, contained at least one reference to Ethel Barrymore's speaking voice, one to the Russian ballet and two to Jeritza. Subsequently they'd had to lift him out of the financial department after he'd included an essay on the art of Bozo Snyder, the burlesque comedian, in a story purporting to tell the fall of the French franc.

"Well," I said, "it looks to me as though he were going to be just as great a loss here."

The way I figured it was that those that knew Saint-Saëns and Schopenhauer didn't know Benny Leonard and Hank Gowdy, and those that knew Benny and Hank didn't care who Saint-Saëns and Schopenhauer were.

I went back to my seat. Down the rail, just next to the Grays' dugout, was Mount. Hanging on the rail, listening to him and all attention, was Smack Riley. They talked until the Grays went out to the field for the first inning.

"Some story you had this morning," I said when Mount came over. Honestly, I couldn't go any further than that.

"Oh!" He seemed surprised. "Glad you liked it." His eyes followed Smack, loping out to right. "That man," he said, "is a genuine artist."

"Smack Riley!" I exclaimed. "Get out! Smack Riley never drew a line in his life!"

He didn't have a word to say to that, of course, for I had him dead to rights. I'd known

48

Smack from the day he reached the Grays' training camp five years before, and if he was an artist then I'm a dry-point etcher.

II

Personally speaking, I'll admit I never saw anything in the way of baseball reporting in my life like that stuff Mount shot over last season. That first day's story was just a hint of what was coming. In August he started that column of his, "In My Humble Opinion," on the sporting page of the *Sphere*. Evidently he had permission to write about anything on this earth; but mostly, I imagine, he was expected to write about sports. Pretty soon it began to look like a serial appreciation of Smack Riley the artist, Smack Riley the aesthete, Smack Riley the Walter Pater of the diamond.

He wrote as if baseball had just been invented. All kinds of art and artistry that everybody had always overlooked, Mount found and wrote about — the way Ty Cobb, whom I usually call the Georgia Peach, started for first; the way Tris Speaker played outfield; the way George Sisler took a high one. Eugene O'Neills of the diamond, Wagners — Richard — of the diamond. And once when he didn't approve of a fellow he wrote that he was the Harold Bell Wright of the diamond, which seemed to be the only thing he could think of to call O'Hara. Next day he came to the Stadium in a nervous sweat.

"Do you suppose," he worried, "that O'Hara will be insulted at what I wrote? I did it, I'm afraid, a little hastily."

I assured him that Tad O'Hara had probably never heard of but three Wrights in his

49

life — one being an old-time second baseman and the two others the aviators.

I read his stuff every day. Practically everything in it was over my head, but — well, it was a curiosity. I'd be the last person in the world to say anything about aesthetics. To a certain extent it is all right, none better, and nobody is a heartier supporter of the arts than I; but when it came to saying, over and over again, how beautiful Smack Riley was when he struck out — well —

The two soon got to be prime buddies, and when the team took the road in May the acquaintanceship took up so much of Smack's time that our three-year-old poker foursome, consisting of Harry Kelly, Matthews, the second-string catcher, Smack and me, was broken up. Smack was out, always, with something very important to talk over, in whispers, with Marshall Mount. They talked all the way to St. Louis that trip, and I'd never have guessed that Smack knew that many words.

They were that way throughout the season. It was art that brought them together. In Washington, Mount took Smack to the Corcoran Art Gallery, in Chicago, to the Chicago Museum. But as long as the old mace, as I called it, whanged away at the ball with as much success as it did, neither I nor Hall Miller, the manager, cared. Artist or no artist, the big bum was hitting 'em straight and hard, day after day, and what a homerun record he was piling up!

50

The sporting writers were, of course, giving a good third of their space to him; but what was funny, one of the highbrow weeklies ran a story about him. Mr. Smack Riley, it was called. By Marshall Mount, of course. It was the same stuff — form, rhythm, grace, force, coordination, beauty.

I got to calling Mount Smack's Boswell. Being literary too, he got it right off, and smiled. But Smack wouldn't take any kidding. "This Mount is a artist," he declared, "a artist of the first water."

We tried a little ragging, but Smack was for busting somebody on the ear.

"Well," I said, "speaking personally, I think you're off your nut." I told him right out, the big bum!

I was sure of it a few days later when I caught him reading *Primal Grace* by a fellow with a name not less than Greek. His face got red.

"If you say anything about this, you big bum," he said, "I'll knock you for a row of stumps." I came right back at him.

"I'm not going to say anything about it, you big bum," I said; "but don't think your threats have anything to do with it, you big bum."

He didn't say anything else, but I didn't want any hard feelings.

"Look here, Smack," I said, "we've been pretty good friends. Let's don't let art come between us. Now what's all this racket?"

Smack laid *Primal Grace* down.

"Mapes," he said, "I reckon the gang is a little sore; but look, Mount's right about this thing. There is an art to baseball. It's got all the qualities of epic drama. Some day people are going to see it and they're going to put up statues to baseball players in museums and things, like the old Greeks put them up to discus players and javelin throwers.

"Mapes," he said, "I've seen the handwriting on the wall. I'm going to get one of them statues. I'm going to get the first one. I'm going to be the first artist of the game, the first native American athaletic artist. I'm giving all my thoughts — "

All of Smack's thoughts!

51

" — all my thoughts to it." He fished into his pocket. "Look here." He handed me some manuscript paper. "See that? That's a part I'm going to play in a show."

I looked at it. It was labeled, *Gods Athirst, a Masque.* A cast of characters, gods, maidens, and Smack's part, Arno, a Rollicking God. I couldn't help it. I've got no more control over my face than the next fellow. I laughed. The peace negotiations fell through.

"Gimme" — Smack was snarling — "gimme that manuscript! What could anybody expect from a boob like you? What d'you know about art, or anything else for that matter? I got a good mind to soak you."

"Go ahead, you big bum," I retorted, but he didn't.

III

By the time the pennant race was in what I called its last stages, Smack was an acknowledged artist. That is, other artists were acknowledging him. To give Mount no more than his due, he certainly sold Smack to the highbrow crowd.

Once they had him down in Greenwich Village to speak on "The Human Body — As it is and as it Should Be." Greenwich Village! And to art students! Personally speaking, the English language means nothing to me. I'm not its protector. It can get in trouble and stay in trouble for all I care. But truly, it's wicked to do things to it that Smack does. It tears my heart out. I'm that sympathetic when Smack gets hold of five words in close succession. For when he gets through with them you couldn't get twenty pfennigs for them, even in the Balkan States, where they need languages so much.

But Smack got away with it. "Gorgeously naive" was the way Mount described it the

52

next day, and "the simple truth of an authentic artist" was what Smack had to say on human grace and rhythm.

Somebody took motion pictures of him. He posed in a tiger skin for a magazine on physical culture. And another magazine, so fine that up to that time it had run nothing but art photographs of Mary Pickford, Billie Burke and Irene Castle, published a full-page mood study of our bucko. A mood study!

And then he made his appearance as Arno a Rollicking God in *Gods Athirst* at the Artists' Playhouse, down in the Village. The Grays had reached town a few days before from the final swing around the circuit. Leading by four games and with the gang playing championship ball every minute, the old gonfalon, as I sometimes call it, seemed sewed up. Smack, the big bum, was whanging away in great shape, with the old homeruns clicking every four or five days and plenty of singles between. It looked pretty rosy for the Grays when the Gulls hit town for the last series of six games. Four games behind the Grays, the Gulls did not look like a very serious menace.

I went early that night to the Artists' Playhouse. Anybody who knows where I rank in artistic circles will be able to tell you whether I got an invitation or not. It was very exclusive, the door man told me, and not even J.P. Morgan himself could get in without an invitation. So that meant, of course, that I had to slip him a simoleon.

The Artists' Playhouse was a dump if ever there was one. If you can imagine a theater different from the Hippodrome in every respect, bar none, you know what the Artists' Playhouse looked like. Mount was already there, down front, talking to a couple of bloods wearing orange ties. I took a back seat, where I wouldn't be seen and thrown out on charges of cleanliness. The place filled up. The audience consisted of frowzy men and

johnson

frowzier women, all smoking cigarettes, and I do not exaggerate when I say that two of them had on horn-rimmed spectacles.

After a while, without any preliminaries, the lights went out. The footlights, following some hesitation, opened their eyes. The curtain went up, revealing, the program said, "At the Foot of the Mountain of the Gods," but I regarded this as a gross exaggeration. On the other hand, I do not know how to describe this scenery other than to say that I have never seen anything like it anywhere, and I have seen almost everything.

Low music first, and then a few girls suffering pitifully from malnutrition and down, apparently, to their last garment, tripped lightly out and hoofed it a bit. They ran hither and thither, being cunning, roguish, playful and what not, and in this festive fashion consumed about five minutes. Then, suddenly, they all prostrated themselves toward the left rear entrance. Somebody blew a bugle. A drum rolled. Then Harry Dudley Riley — by the program — entered.

He entered slowly, taking long steps, being stealthy, just like a milk wagon. He was next to naked, but composed. He looked around slowly at first and then began to rollick. He waved his arms, and one of them was so unfortunate as to catch a lightly clad maiden under the chin, lifting her off her feet. She sat down heavily, with an astonished look on her face. I laughed, but nobody else did. Smack didn't notice; he was very intent on his rollicking.

He paused occasionally to raise a clenched fist at the chandelier and swear, by pantomime, a mighty oath to the gods athirst, but mostly he played tag with the gals. I confess here and now that I do not know much about dancing. Frisco, Pat Rooney, Eddie Leonard, Harry Greb — they're about my speed. But without looking it up in the books, I'm willing

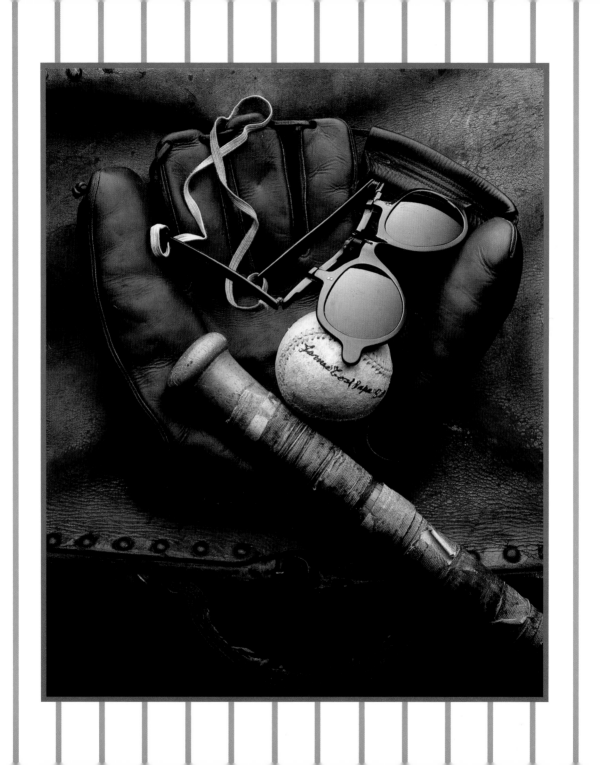

to risk a small sum, say, ten simoleans, that Smack Riley did everything wrong that it is possible to do on two feet except fall into the orchestra. I couldn't have laughed more heartily if I'd just seen an umpire shot.

The highbrows, though, were enthralled. They must have been ready to believe anything they read in the *Sphere*, for the only way Smack could have been worse would have been by wearing a fire bucket on each foot. He'd knocked down half the scenery before he was through, and there wasn't a girl on stage that didn't have the fear of God in her eyes as she heard the galumph-galumph of Smack Riley's bare Number 12's pounding playfully along behind her.

Then it ended. Arno backed into what was left of the scenery, stepped on a rope, tripped and dived into the wings. Speaking personally, I hoped he'd been knocked unconscious, for I, at any rate, still had some pride in the good old masculine sex. He didn't come out again, even to acknowledge the applause, which was good and loud. They called him bravo. And the next time I saw Smack he had his shirt and pants on and was thanking the audience individually, as he made his way to the door, for their kind appreciation.

I listened in, eavesdropped on some of the talk: "Primitive genius . . . astounding sense of grace . . . liquid movements . . . crude brilliance . . . a sparkle of greatness ever present . . . a reserve strength."

56

IV

It was a great day for baseball when the Gulls and Grays took the field. The Stadium was packed. Forty thousand people if there was a bat boy — and there was a bat boy. The

Grays, fighting sportsmen every one of them, smelled the World Series receipts; and the Gulls, just as true disciples of all that is highest and finest in sport, were also thinking about the jack that might be theirs. Both teams were keyed up, snappy, and the crowd soon showed that it was prepared to roar its lungs out.

I looked for Smack. He was at the rail talking to Marshall Mount again, and somehow the sight depressed me, gave me a feeling that all was not well. Of course I had no reason for believing that the exhibition of the night before had cured the Smacker, but I did, at the bottom, have some hope that it had.

Presently he pried himself loose from Mount and, with the rest of the Grays, went out for fielding practice. It was then I saw that something was indeed wrong, and as near as I could figure it, the Smacker was still dizzy with art. For at the first fungo he exhibited some strange and, to me, incomprehensible didos. He started for the ball with long, stealthy strides, his arms swaying rhythmically with the swing of his body — and his body swung wickedly. It was a curious galumph and it served to bring him where the ball came down exactly forty-five seconds after the ball was down.

One of the boys in the press box chuckled.

"Who does that bum think he is, Gertrude Hoffman?" The open bleachers threw back its head and bayed at the sun. "Nick Altrock's got nothing on that bird!" Everybody had noticed it; but only Mount and I, it seemed, had an inkling of the explanation; and Mount, the fathead, appeared anything but dissatisfied.

The second fungo he could have taken in his tracks. Instead, he chose to run gracefully around in a circle, swinging his arms most beautifully, and the ball nearly landed on his bean. The bleachers roared. Good old Smack Riley was being funny for them! Good old Smack!

57

It might have been Greek, all right, but it wasn't baseball.

Then the game started. Rush worked for the Grays and Rocker hurled for the Gulls, and for five innings they put up what I would call a corking pitchers' battle. It was three up, three down, with only now and then a fluky bingle getting a man on one of the hassocks. And during that time the owner of the splendid body in the right field was given no opportunity to do anything with it. At bat he got one hit, a single, and was left on first. It was not until the first half of the sixth that anything happened for the records.

Hoban, first up for the Gulls, beat out a bunt. Then he stole second. Barber sent a slow roller to short and Hoban made third on the out. This wasn't so good, but time would tell, as I have said so many times. And then Heinie Schmidt raised a fly to right, directly at the old reliable Smack Riley.

Everything else being even, I would have breathed a sigh of relief, but nothing else was even. I wanted to close my eyes, but I didn't. Maybe — perhaps — there was a chance that the big bum's eye would be working and his mean right arm prepared for the shot to the plate if Hoban tried to score after the catch, but —

I watched Smack, together with forty thousand others, while he moved stealthily backward and forward, waving his arms to the tempo of the "Humoresque," under that falling ball. Hoban was holding third by a toe, ready to dash for the plate if anything happened.

And then Smack caught it — caught it somewhere around his left shoulder blade. Not a graceful catch, perhaps, but it would do. And in the same second a roar swept the stands. Hoban had started for the plate — a desperate chance for a run that might mean the game.

Then Smack whipped back his arm, his eye on the plate and the speeding Hoban. He took a long, slow step, and at that instant I realized that it wasn't Smack out there, but

Arno the Rollicking God. His hand went back nearly to the ground. He hopped once or twice like a shot putter, and finally, with a sinuous movement, he got rid of the ball toward the plate. By the time it reached the catcher, Hoban had crossed the plate, gone to the dugout and written a postcard to his cousin in Duluth, Minnesota.

There was what I would call pandemonium, mostly in the form of boos for the Smacker; but he appeared undisturbed, his art still intact. Three seats to my left Mount spoke:

"That pose was astoundingly like the Discus Thrower, don't you think? Just a flash, a haunting touch of beauty."

That one tally looked as big as seven, for it ended all scoring for the time being. It was again one-two-three in the sixth and seventh, with Rush pitching first-rate ball. In fact one run began to look as though it were all that was going to be necessary.

But in the eighth the Grays snapped out of it. Rush, whose last recorded hit occurred the year Tris Speaker got his first gray hair, socked one into left field and it was good for a single. Harrigan grounded out to first, Rush taking second. Then Rocker skyrocketed, walking Massey and Hedges on eight straight balls.

Boom! The roar started. The break was here and the crowd realized it. The Grays were swarming out of their dugout, crouching on the grass, barking across the swell of the infield at the runners. There was a tightening among the Gulls. The infielders leaned a little farther forward. The drive was coming and they were ready to meet it.

The formless surge of sound, rolling in mass volume over the field, began to settle into a steady thump-thump, a pounding of feet, as forty thousand people caught the thrill.

And then the Smacker crawled out of the trench, caught up three bats and started for the plate. The bases full and the king up! Forgotten was that slow throw home. This was

59

the minute! This was drama — epic drama!

Smack Riley swung his clubs slowly while Rocker and Dowden conferred. Then he tossed two of them aside and stepped into the batter's box. He dug his cleats in the dirt, got a toe hold, waved his wagon tongue. Dowden, his mask adjusted, squatted, and Rocker tried his first, a curve over the outside, low.

Wow!

The Smacker had larruped it down the third-base line for a mile, into the bleachers — foul by inches. Rocker had nearly fainted. And when he saw Harry Lannigan, the Gulls' manager, waving to him from the dugout that his bath was ready, he smiled a happy smile. He did not even wait to see who was coming from the bull pen to relieve him.

A smallish figure had separated himself from the warmers-up down by the exit gate and was coming slowly across the field. Smack, accustomed to such changes, leaned carelessly on his bat, resting his rhythm for a few seconds. He might well have been an actor posing in a hired dress suit. The smallish figure neared the diamond, and the Smacker, noting it for the first time, straightened up suddenly.

"Mulligan," bawled the announcer, "now pitching for the Gulls!"

A newcomer to the league, Mulligan was small, terrifically ugly, red-haired and gnarled in appearance, and he chewed on the world's largest cud of tobacco. He sauntered into this breach coolly. And with the bases full, Smack Riley at the bat, forty thousand people storming and a pennant not far in the future — it was what I would refer to as a tight pinch.

But it was the Smacker, and not Mulligan, who seemed dumbfounded. His eyes were frozen on the little pitcher, now tossing a practice ball to Dowden. And Mulligan's ruddy

60

Winchester
Kraher 2b
Mullins 1b
Kirchen
Ried
Long lf
Cramer rf
Schultz c
Wright p
1902
AT THE
CINCINNATI
BALL
Umpire Hanley July 19-1910.

face was worth a look or two as it shifted shapes regularly with the grinding of his tobacco. The Smacker was paralyzed. Nor did he move until Tim Hurley, the umpire at the plate, called him.

"This ain't no hotel lobby," he said.

The Banzai of Bingle, as I called him once, momentarily regained life. With a nervous jerk he stepped forward and swung his bat tentatively. But it died down slowly, and the forty thousand pounded, pounded, pounded, roaring — roaring for blood. Then Mulligan began to wind up.

I myself, a veteran of the press box, the dean of sporting writers, have never seen anything like that wind-up, and, as I say, I have seen pretty nearly everything. But Mulligan! He involved himself in a chaos of arms and legs that showed no signs whatever of solution. His right arm swung three times and then plunged squarely through.

He slapped himself in the face with his left foot. He laid his thorax on the pitcher's plate. He revolved his head four times, strangled himself with his elbows, bit the back of his right knee, got both feet off the ground at the same time, remained stationary in the air, and finally, at the height of the maneuver, exuded the ball, it emerging, strangely enough, from his Adam's apple.

It was a strike. The Smacker did not even lift his bat from his shoulder, though the ball split the plate. He was paralyzed again; and if he'd been only a little more lifelike he might have passed for a statue — Athlete Dumbfounded.

Mulligan got the ball back and the same thing happened again. This time the ball appeared from the small of his back, but, wherever it came from, it proved to be another strike all the same.

johnson

The Stadium stood up, boomed its call to the four ends of Harlem.

The Smacker stood oblivious of his demise. His glazed eyes remained on Mulligan and, as he watched, the red-haired pitcher shifted the tumor of plug cut from the right side of his head to the left. The shape of his whole superstructure was altered. Whereas there had been a goiter on the right side, there was then a wen on the left. It was astounding — and terrible. And then there was a sudden higher roar. The Smacker had crumpled to the ground in a swoon.

V

Readers, the rest is eyewitness stuff corroborated by the records and explainable by psychology.

You don't remember who finished second in the league last year, for nobody ever remembers who finished second; but I'll tell you. It was the Grays.

There was another inning to this game I've described, to be sure, and five other games to be played, but this is one of those things stranger and more tragic than fiction. I could have made this the final game of the season, and it the deciding game, too, but these are facts.

When they took the heart out of Smack Riley they took the heart out of the Grays, and after that they played with all the skill of nine Bulgars. But as I said, I'm only a plain man, just a reporter, and not a dramatic critic, as Mount is now, or even a psychologist, so I can account for what happened only by what I saw and heard.

I was present when Smack was brought back to life. I saw the baffled and tortured look in his eyes, the look which remained there throughout the series. I was present when he uttered his first words on regaining consciousness, the only words that he ever uttered on the subject. They were poignant sounds, rising from the soul of a tormented Arno.

"That," he said slowly, thoughtfully, shuddering again at the very thought, "was the most unaesthetic thing I ever seen."

I witnessed also his pitiful trips to the plate, a broken man, with scarcely life enough to lift his bat, and his doleful trips back to the bench. And I was there at the end of the sixth game — the sixth game the Grays had lost in succession, the pennant gone — when the first original thought the Smacker ever had came into his head with dazzling clearness. It was prompted by a remark from Harrison, the center fielder.

"Well, Smack," he said, "it's all over, and you'll not get that superheterodyne radio set you said you was, the first day of the season, outa the series money."

The Smacker rose suddenly. A gleam of understanding came into his eyes, the first, I suppose, in years. He crawled out of the dugout, selected a bat carefully and then straightened up. His arm went back, less like Arno than anything he'd done in weeks, and in a flash a long black bat whirred through the air straight at the press box.

"There's too damned much aesthetics going on round here!"

The bat reached Mount, but the words didn't. It caught him on the ear, and now he is the only dramatic critic in New York with a cauliflower ear.

64

And these, readers, are the facts, the evidence on which I accuse Marshall Mount of the *Sphere* and Smack Riley of the Grays.

bush league hero

Any man who can look handsome in a dirty baseball suit is an Adonis. There is something about the baggy pants, and the Micawber-shaped collar, and the skull-fitting cap, and the foot or so of tan, blue, or pink undershirt sleeve sticking out at the arms, that just naturally kills a man's best points. Then too, a baseball suit requires so much in the matter of leg. Therefore, when I say that Rudie Schlachweiler was a dream even in his baseball uniform, with a dirty brown streak right up the side of the pants where he had slid for base, you may know that the girls camped on the grounds during the season.

During the summer months our ball park is to us what the Grand Prix is to Paris, or Ascot is to London. What care we that Evers gets seven thousand a year (or is it a month?); or that Chicago's new Southside ball park seats thirty-five thousand (or is it million?).

edna ferber

Of what interest are such meager items compared with the knowledge that "Pug" Coulan, who plays short, goes with Undine Meyers, the girl up there in the eighth row, with the pink dress and the red roses on her hat? When "Pug" snatches a high one out of the firmament we yell with delight, and even as we yell we turn sideways to look up and see how Undine is taking it. Undine's shining eyes are fixed on "Pug," and he knows it, stoops to brush the dust off his dirt-begrimed baseball pants, takes an attitude of careless grace and misses the next play.

Our grandstand seats almost two thousand, counting the boxes. But only the snobs, and the girls with new hats, sit in the boxes. Box seats are comfortable, it is true, and they cost only an additional ten cents, but we have come to consider them undemocratic, and unworthy of true fans. Mrs. Freddy Van Dyne, who spends her winters in Egypt and sum- mers at the ball park, comes out to the game every afternoon in her automobile, but she never occupies a box seat; so why should we? She perches up in the grandstand with the rest of the enthusiasts, and when Kelley puts one over she stands up and clinches her fists, and waves her arms and shouts with the best of 'em. She has even been known to cry, "Good eye! Good eye!" when things were at a fever heat. The only really blasé individual in the ball park is Willie Grimes, who peddles ice-cream cones. For that matter, I once saw Willie turn a languid head to pipe, in his thin voice, "Give 'em a dark one, Dutch! Give 'em a dark one!"

Well, that will do for the fresh dash of local color. Now for the story.

Ivy Keller came home June nineteenth from Miss Shont's select school for young ladies. By June twenty-first she was bored limp. You could hardly see the plaits of her white tailored shirtwaist for fraternity pins and secret society emblems, and her bedroom

66

was ablaze with college banners and pennants to such an extent that the maid gave notice every Thursday — which was upstairs cleaning day.

For two weeks after her return Ivy spent most of her time writing letters and waiting for them, and reading the classics on the front porch, dressed in a middy blouse and a blue skirt, with her hair done in a curly Greek effect like the girls on the covers of the *Ladies' Magazine*. She posed against the canvas bosom of the porch chair with one foot under her, the other swinging free, showing a tempting thing in beaded slipper, silk stocking, and what the story writers call "slim ankle."

On the second Saturday after her return her father came home for dinner at noon, found her deep in Volume Two of *Les Miserables*.

"Whew! This is a scorcher!" he exclaimed, and dropped down on a wicker chair next to Ivy. Ivy looked at her father with languid interest, and smiled a daughterly smile. Ivy's father was an insurance man, alderman of his ward, president of the Civic Improvement Club, member of five lodges, and an habitual delegate.

"Aren't you feeling well, Ivy?" he asked. "Looking a little pale. It's the heat, I suppose. Gosh! Something smells good. Run in and tell Mother I'm here."

Ivy kept one slender finger between the leaves of her book. "I'm perfectly well," she replied. "That must be beefsteak and onions. Ugh!" And she shuddered, and went indoors.

68

Dad Keller looked after her thoughtfully. Then he went in, washed his hands, and sat down at the table with Ivy and her mother.

"Just a sliver for me," said Ivy, "and no onions."

Her father put down his knife and fork, cleared his throat, and spake, thus:

ferber

"You get on your hat and meet me at the 2:45 inter-urban. You're going to the ball game with me."

"Ball game!" repeated Ivy. "I? But I'd — "

"Yes, you do," interrupted her father. "You've been moping around here looking a cross between Saint Cecelia and Little Eva long enough. I don't care if you don't know a spitball from a fadeaway when you see it. You'll be out in the air all afternoon, and there'll be some excitement. All the girls go. You'll like it. They're playing Marshalltown."

Ivy went, looking the sacrificial lamb. Five minutes after the game was called she pointed one tapering white finger in the direction of the pitcher's mound.

"Who's that?" she asked.

"Pitcher," explained Papa Keller, laconically. Then, patiently: "He throws the ball."

"Oh," said Ivy. "What did you say his name was?"

"I didn't say. But it's Rudie Schlachweiler. The boys call him Dutch. Kind of a pet, Dutch is."

"Rudie Schlachweiler!" murmured Ivy, dreamily. "What a strong name!"

"Want some peanuts?" inquired her father.

"Does one eat peanuts at a ball game?"

"It ain't hardly legal if you don't," Pa Keller assured her.

"Two sacks," said Ivy. "Papa, why do they call it a diamond, and what are those brown bags at the corners, and what does it count if you hit the ball, and why do they rub their hands in the dust and then — er — spit on them, and what salary does a pitcher get, and why does the red-haired man on the other side dance around like that

69

between the second and third brown bag, and doesn't a pitcher do anything but pitch, and wh — ?"

"You're on," said Papa.

After that Ivy didn't miss a game during all the time that the team played in the home town. She went without a new hat, and didn't care whether Jean Valjean got away with the goods or not, and forgot whether you played third hand high or low in bridge. She even became chummy with Undine Meyers, who wasn't her kind of a girl at all. Undine was thin in a voluptuous kind of way, if such a paradox can be, and she had red lips, and a roving eye, and she ran around downtown without a hat more than was strictly necessary. But Undine and Ivy had two subjects in common. They were baseball and love. It is queer how the limelight will make heroes of us all.

Now "Pug" Coulan, who was red-haired, and had shoulders like an ox, and arms that hung down to his knees, like those of an orangoutan, slaughtered beeves at the Chicago stockyards in the winter. In the summer he slaughtered hearts. He wore mustard-colored shirts that matched his hair, and his baseball stockings generally had a rip in them somewhere, but when he was on the diamond we were almost ashamed to look at Undine, so wholly did her heart shine in her eyes.

Now, we'll have just another dash or two of local color. In a small town the chances for hero worship are few. If it weren't for the traveling men our girls wouldn't know whether stripes or checks were the thing in gents' suitings. When the baseball season opened the girls swarmed on it. Those that didn't understand baseball pretended they did. When the team was out of town our form of greeting was changed from, "Good morning!" or "Howdy-do!" to "What's the score?" Every night the results of the games throughout the

70

ferber

league were posted up on the blackboard in front of Schlager's hardware store, and to see the way in which the crowd stood around it, and streamed across the street toward it, you'd have thought they were giving away gas stoves and hammock couches.

Going home in the street car after the game the girls used to gaze adoringly at the dirty faces of their sweat-begrimed heroes, and then they'd rush home, have supper, change their dresses, do their hair, and rush downtown past the Parker Hotel to mail their letters. The baseball boys boarded over at the Griggs House, which is third-class, but they used their toothpicks, and held the post-mortem of the day's game out in front of the Parker Hotel, which is our leading hostelry. The post office receipts record for our town was broken during the months of June, July, and August.

Mrs. Freddy Van Dyne started the trouble by having the team over to dinner, "Pug" Coulan and all. After all, why not? No foreign and impecunious princes penetrate as far inland as our town. They get only as far as New York, or Newport, where they are gobbled up by many-moneyed matrons. If Mrs. Freddy Van Dyne found the supply of available lions limited, why should she not try to content herself with a jackal or so?

Ivy was asked. Until then she had contented herself with gazing at her hero. She had become such a hardened baseball fan that she followed the game with a score card, accurately jotting down every play.

She sat next to Rudie at dinner. Before she had nibbled her second salted almond, Ivy Keller and Rudie Schlachweiler understood each other. Rudie illustrated certain plays by drawing lines on the tablecloth with his knife and Ivy gazed, wide-eyed, and allowed her soup to grow cold.

The first night that Rudie called, Pa Keller thought it a great joke. He sat out on the

ferber

porch with Rudie and Ivy and talked baseball, and got up to show Rudie how he could have got the goat of that Keokuk catcher. Rudie looked politely interested, and laughed in all the right places. But Ivy didn't need to pretend. Rudie Schlachweiler spelled baseball to her. She did not think of her caller as a good-looking young man in a blue serge suit. Even as he sat there she saw him as a blonde god standing on the pitcher's mound, with the scars of battle on his baseball pants, his left foot placed in front of him at right angles with his right foot, his gaze fixed on first base in a cunning effort to deceive the man at bat, in that favorite attitude of pitchers just before they get ready to swing their left leg and heist one over.

The second time that Rudie called, Ma Keller said:

"Ivy, I don't like that ball player coming here to see you. The neighbors'll talk."

The third time Rudie called, Pa Keller said: "What's that guy doing here again?"

The fourth time Rudie called, Pa Keller and Ma Keller said, in unison: "This thing has got to stop."

But it didn't. It had had too good a start. For the rest of the season Ivy met her knight of the sphere around the corner. Theirs was a walking courtship. They used to roam up as far as the State Road, and down as far as the river, and Rudie would fain have talked of love, but Ivy talked of baseball.

"Darling," Rudie would murmur, pressing Ivy's arm closer, "when did you first begin to care?"

"Why I liked the very first game I saw when Dad — "

"I mean, when did you first begin to care for me?"

"Oh! When you put three men out in that game with Marshalltown when the teams

were tied in the eighth inning. Remember? Say, Rudie dear, what was the matter with your arm today? You let three men walk, and Albia's weakest hitter got a homerun out of you."

"Oh, forget baseball for a minute, Ivy! Let's talk about something else. Let's talk about — us."

"Us? Well, you're baseball, aren't you?" retorted Ivy. "And if you are, I am. Did you notice the way that Ottumwa man pitched yesterday? He didn't do any acting for the grandstand. He didn't reach up above his head, and wrap his right shoulder with his left toe, and swing his arm three times and then throw seven inches outside the plate. He just took the ball in his hand, looked at it curiously for a moment, and fired it — zing! — like that, over the plate. I'd get that ball if I were you."

"Isn't this a grand night?" murmured Rudie.

"But they didn't have a hitter in the bunch," went on Ivy. "And not a man in the team could run. That's why they're tail-enders. Just the same, that man on the mound was a wizard, and if he had one decent player to give him some support — "

Well, the thing came to a climax. One evening, two weeks before the close of the season, Ivy put on her hat and announced that she was going downtown to mail her letters.

"Mail your letters in the daytime," growled Papa Keller.

"I didn't have time today," answered Ivy. "It was a thirteen-inning game, and it lasted until six o'clock."

It was then that Papa Keller banged the heavy fist of decision down on the library table.

74

"This thing's got to stop!" he thundered. "I won't have any girl of mine running the streets with a ball player, understand? Now you quit seeing this seventy-five-dollars-a-month bush leaguer or leave this house. I mean it."

"All right," said Ivy, with a white calm. "I'll leave. I can make the grandest kind of angel-food with marshmallow icing, and you know yourself my fudges can't be equaled. He'll be playing in the major leagues in three years. Why just yesterday there was a strange man at the game — a city man, you could tell by his hat band, and the way his clothes were cut. He stayed through the whole game, and never took his eyes off Rudie. I just know he was a scout for the Cubs."

"Probably a hardware drummer, or a fellow that Schlachweiler owes money to."

Ivy began to pin on her hat. A scared look leaped into Papa Keller's eyes. He looked a little old, too, and drawn, at that minute. He stretched forth a rather tremulous hand.

"Ivy — girl," he said.

"What?" snapped Ivy.

"Your old father's just talking for your own good. You're breaking your ma's heart. You and me have been good pals, haven't we?"

"Yes," said Ivy, grudgingly, and without looking up.

"Well now, look here. I've got a proposition to make to you. The season's over in two more weeks. The last week they play out of town. Then the boys'll come back for a week or so, just to hang around town and try to get used to the idea of leaving us. Then they'll scatter to take up their winter jobs — cutting ice, most of 'em," he added, grimly.

"Mr. Schlachweiler is employed in a large establishment in Slatersville, Ohio," said

Ivy, with dignity. "He regards baseball as his profession, and he cannot do anything that would affect his pitching arm."

Pa Keller put on the tremolo stop and and brought a misty look into his eyes.

"Ivy, you'll do one last thing for your old father, won't you?"

"Maybe," answered Ivy, coolly.

"Don't make that fellow any promises. Now wait a minute! Let me get through. I won't put any crimp in your plans. I won't speak to Schlachweiler. Promise you won't do anything rash until the ball season's over. Then we'll wait just one month, see? Till along about November. Then if you feel like you want to see him — "

"But how — "

"Hold on. You mustn't write to him, or see him, or let him write to you during that time, see? Then, if you feel the way you do now, I'll take you to Slatersville to see him. Now that's fair, ain't it? Only don't let him know you're coming."

"M-m-m-yes," said Ivy.

"Shake hands on it." She did. Then she left the room with a rush, headed in the direction of her own bedroom. Pa Keller treated himself to a prodigious wink and went out to the vegetable garden in search of Mother.

The team went out on the road, lost five games, won two, and came home in fourth place. For a week they lounged around the Parker Hotel and held up the street corners downtown, took many farewell drinks, then, slowly, by ones and twos, they left for the packing houses, freight depots, and gents' furnishing stores from whence they came.

October came in with a blaze of sumac and oak leaves. Ivy stayed home and learned to make veal loaf and apple pies. The worry lines around Pa Keller's face began to deepen. Ivy said that she didn't believe that she cared to go back to Miss Shont's select school for young ladies.

October thirty-first came.

"We'll take the eight-fifteen tomorrow," said her father to Ivy.

"All right," said Ivy.

"Do you know where he works?" asked he.

"No," answered Ivy.

"That'll be all right. I took the trouble to look him up last August."

The short November afternoon was drawing to its close (as our best talent would put it) when Ivy and her father walked along the streets of Slatersville. (I can't tell you what streets, because I don't know.) Pa Keller brought up before a narrow little shoe shop.

"Here we are," he said, and ushered Ivy in. A short, stout, proprietary figure approached them smiling a mercantile smile.

"What can I do for you?" he inquired.

Ivy's eyes searched the shop for a tall, golden-haired form in a soiled baseball suit.

"We'd like to see a gentleman named Schlachweiler — Rudolph Schlachweiler," said Pa Keller.

"Anything very special?" inquired the proprietor. "He's — rather busy just now. Wouldn't anybody else do? Of course, if — "

"No," growled Keller.

The boss turned. "Hi! Schlachweiler!" he bawled toward the rear of the dim little shop.

77

"Yessir," answered a muffled voice.

"Front!" yelled the boss, and withdrew to a safe listening distance.

A vaguely troubled look lurked in the depths of Ivy's eyes. From behind the partition of the rear of the shop emerged a tall figure. It was none other than our hero. He was in his shirt-sleeves, and he struggled into his coat as he came forward, wiping his mouth with the back of his hand, hurriedly, and swallowing.

I have said that the shop was dim. Ivy and her father stood at one side, their backs to the light. Rudie came forward, rubbing his hands together in the manner of clerks.

"Something in shoes?" he politely inquired.

Then he saw.

"Ivy! — ah — Miss Keller!" he exclaimed. Then, awkwardly: "Well, how-do, Mr. Keller. I certainly am glad to see you both. How's the old town? What are you doing in Slatersville?"

"Why — Ivy — " began Pa Keller, blunderingly.

But Ivy clutched his arm with a warning hand. The vaguely troubled look in her eyes had become wildly so.

"Schlachweiler!" shouted the voice of the boss. "Customers!" and he waved a hand in the direction of the fitting benches.

"All right, sir," answered Rudie. "Just a minute."

78

"Dad had to come on business," said Ivy, hurriedly. "And he brought me with him. I'm — I'm on my way to school in Cleveland, you know. Awfully glad to have seen you again. We must go. That lady wants her shoes, I'm sure, and your employer is glaring at us. Come, Dad."

ferber

At the door she turned just in time to see Rudie removing the shoe from the pudgy foot of the fat lady customer.

We'll take a jump of six months. That brings us into the lap of April.

Pa Keller looked up from his evening paper. Ivy, home for Easter vacation, was at the piano. Ma Keller was sewing.

Pa Keller cleared his throat. "I see by the paper," he announced, "that Schlachweiler's been sold to Des Moines. Too bad we lost him. He was a great little pitcher, but he played in bad luck. Whenever he was on the slab the boys seemed to give him poor support."

"Fudge!" exclaimed Ivy, continuing to play, but turning a spirited face toward her father. "What piffle! Whenever a player pitches rotten ball you'll always hear him howling about the support he didn't get. Schlachweiler was a bum pitcher. Anybody could hit him with a willow wand, on a windy day, with the sun in his eyes."

baseball hattie

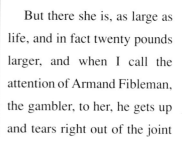

It comes on springtime, and the little birdies are singing in the trees in Central Park, and the grass is green all around and about, and I am at the Polo Grounds on the opening day of the baseball season, when who do I behold but Baseball Hattie. I am somewhat surprised at this spectacle, as it is years since I see Baseball Hattie, and for all I know she long ago passes to a better and happier world.

But there she is, as large as life, and in fact twenty pounds larger, and when I call the attention of Armand Fibleman, the gambler, to her, he gets up and tears right out of the joint as if he sees a ghost, for if there is one thing Armand Fibleman loathes and despises, it is a ghost.

I can see that Baseball Hattie is greatly changed, and to tell the truth, I can see that she is getting to be nothing but an old bag.

damon runyon

runyon

Her hair that is once as black as a yard up a stovepipe is gray, and she is wearing gold-rimmed cheaters, although she seems to be pretty well dressed and looks as if she may be in the money a little bit, at that.

But the greatest change in her is the way she sits there very quiet all afternoon, never once opening her yap, even when many of the customers around her are claiming that Umpire William Klem is Public Enemy No. 1 to 16 inclusive, because they think he calls a close one against the Giants. I am wondering if maybe Baseball Hattie is stricken dumb somewhere back down the years, because I can remember when she is usually making speeches in the grandstand in favor of hanging such characters as Umpire William Klem when they call close ones against the Giants. But Hattie just sits there as if she is in a church while the public clamor goes on about her, and she does not as much as cry out robber, or even you big bum at Umpire William Klem.

I see many a baseball bug in my time, male and female, but without doubt the worst bug of them all is Baseball Hattie, and you can say it again. She is most particularly a bug about the Giants, and she never misses a game they play at the Polo Grounds, and in fact she sometimes bobs up watching them play in other cities, which is always very embarrassing to the Giants, as they fear the customers in these cities may get the wrong impression of New York womanhood after listening to Baseball Hattie awhile.

82   The first time I ever see Baseball Hattie to pay any attention to her is in Philadelphia, a matter of twenty-odd years back, when the Giants are playing a series there, and many citizens of New York, including Armand Fibleman and myself, are present, because the Philadelphia customers are great hands for betting on baseball games in those days, and Armand Fibleman figures he may knock a few of them in the creek.

runyon

Armand Fibleman is a character who will bet on baseball games from who-laid-the-chunk, and in fact will bet on anything whatever, because Armand Fibleman is a gambler by trade and has been such since infancy. Personally, I will not bet you four dollars on a baseball game, because in the first place I am not apt to have four dollars, and in the second place I consider horse races a much sounder investment, but I often go around and about with Armand Fibleman, as he is a friend of mine, and sometimes he gives me a little piece of one of his bets for nothing.

Well, what happens in Philadelphia but the umpire forfeits the game in the seventh inning to the Giants by a score of nine to nothing when the Phillies are really leading by five runs, and the reason the umpire takes this action is because he orders several of the Philadelphia players to leave the field for calling him a scoundrel and a rat and a snake in the grass, and also a baboon, and they refuse to take their departure, as they still have more names to call him.

Right away the Philadelphia customers become infuriated in a manner you will scarcely believe, for ordinarily a Philadelphia baseball customer is as quiet as a lamb, no matter what you do to him, and in fact in those days a Philadelphia baseball customer is only considered as somebody to do something to.

But these Philadelphia customers are so infuriated that they not only chase the umpire under the stand, but they wait in the street outside the baseball orchard until the Giants change into their street clothes and come out of the clubhouse. Then the Philadelphia customers begin pegging rocks, and one thing and another, at the Giants, and it is a most exciting and disgraceful scene that is spoken of for years afterwards.

Well, the Giants march along toward the North Philly station to catch a train for home,

83

dodging the rocks and one thing and another the best they can, and wondering why the Philadelphia gendarmes do not come to the rescue, until somebody notices several gendarmes among the customers doing some of the throwing themselves, so the Giants realize that this is a most inhospitable community, to be sure.

Finally all of them get inside the North Philly station and are safe, except a big, tall, left-handed pitcher by the name of Haystack Duggeler, who just reports to the club the day before and who finds himself surrounded by quite a posse of these infuriated Philadelphia customers, and who is unable to make them understand that he is nothing but a rookie, because he has a Missouri accent, and besides, he is half paralyzed with fear.

One of the infuriated Philadelphia customers is armed with a brickbat and is just moving forward to maim Haystack Duggeler with this instrument, when who steps into the situation but Baseball Hattie, who is also on her way to the station to catch a train, and who is greatly horrified by the assault on the Giants.

She seizes the brickbat from the infuriated Philadelphia customer's grasp, and then tags the customer smack-dab between the eyes with his own weapon, knocking him so unconscious that I afterwards hear he does not recover for two weeks, and that he remains practically an imbecile the rest of his days.

Then Baseball Hattie cuts loose on the other infuriated Philadelphia customers with language that they never before hear in those parts, causing them to disperse without further ado, and after the last customer is beyond the sound of her voice, she takes Haystack Duggeler by the pitching arm and personally escorts him to the station.

Now out of this incident is born a wonderful romance between Baseball Hattie and Haystack Duggeler, and in fact it is no doubt love at first sight, and about this period

84

runyon

Haystack Duggeler begins burning up the league with his pitching, and at the same time giving Manager Mac plenty of headaches, including the romance with Baseball Hattie, because anybody will tell you that a left-hander is tough enough on a manager without a romance, and especially a romance with Baseball Hattie.

It seems that the trouble with Hattie is she is in business up in Harlem, and this business consists of a boarding and rooming house where ladies and gentlemen board and room, and personally I never see anything out of line in the matter, but the rumor somehow gets around, as rumors will do, that in the first place, it is not a boarding and rooming house, and in the second place that the ladies and gentlemen who room and board there are by no means ladies and gentlemen, and especially ladies.

Well, this rumor becomes a terrible knock to Baseball Hattie's social reputation. Furthermore, I hear Manager Mac sends for her and requests her to kindly lay off his ballplayers, and especially off a character who can make a baseball sing high C like Haystack Duggeler. In fact, I hear Manager Mac gives her such a lecture on her civic duty to New York and to the Giants that Baseball Hattie sheds tears, and promises she will never give Haystack another tumble the rest of the season.

"You know me, Mac," Baseball Hattie says. "You know I will cut off my nose rather than do anything to hurt your club. I sometimes figure I am in love with this big bloke, but," she says, "maybe it is only gas pushing up around my heart. I will take something for it. To hell with him, Mac!" she says.

So she does not see Haystack Duggeler again, except at a distance, for a long time, and he goes on to win fourteen games in a row, pitching a no-hitter and four two-hitters among them, and hanging up a reputation as a great pitcher, and also as a hundred-percent heel.

86

runyon

Haystack Duggeler is maybe twenty-five at this time, and he comes to the big league with more bad habits than anybody in the history of the world is able to acquire in such a short time. He is especially a great rumpot, and after he gets going good in the league, he is just as apt to appear for a game all mulled up as not.

He is fond of all forms of gambling, such as playing cards and shooting craps, but after they catch him with a deck of readers in a poker game and a pair of tops in a crap game, none of the Giants will play with him any more, except of course when there is nobody else to play with.

He is ignorant about many little things, such as reading and writing and geography and mathematics, as Haystack Duggeler himself admits he never goes to school any more than he can help, but he is so wise when it comes to larceny that I always figure they must have great tutors back in Haystack's old home town of Boonville, Mo.

And no smarter jobbie ever breathes than Haystack when he is out there pitching. He has so much speed that he just naturally throws the ball past a batter before he can get the old musket off his shoulder, and along with his hard one, Haystack has a curve like the letter Q. With two ounces of brains, Haystack Duggeler will be the greatest pitcher that ever lives.

Well, as far as Baseball Hattie is concerned, she keeps her word about not seeing Haystack, although sometimes when he is mulled up he goes around to her boarding and rooming house, and tries to break down the door.

On the days when Haystack Duggeler is pitching, she is always in her favorite seat back of third, and while she roots hard for the Giants no matter who is pitching, she puts on the extra steam when Haystack is bending them over, and it is quite an experience to hear a lady crying lay them in there, Haystack, old boy, and strike this big tramp out, Haystack, and other exclamations of a similar nature, which please Haystack quite some, but annoy Baseball Hattie's neighbors back of third base, such as Armand Fibleman, if he happens to be betting on the other club.

A month before the close of his first season in the big league, Haystack Duggeler gets so ornery that Manager Mac suspends him, hoping maybe it will cause Haystack to do a little thinking, but naturally Haystack is unable to do this, because he has nothing to think with. About a week later, Manager Mac gets to noticing how he can use a few ball games, so he starts looking for Haystack Duggeler, and finds him tending bar on Eighth Avenue with his uniform hung up back of the bar as an advertisement.

The baseball writers speak of Haystack as an eccentric, which is a polite way of saying he is a screwball, but they consider him a most unique character and are always writing humorous stories about him, though any one of them will lay you plenty of nine to five that Haystack winds up an umbay. The chances are they will raise their price a little, as the season closes and Haystack is again under suspension with cold weather coming on and not a dime in his pants pockets.

It is sometime along in the winter that Baseball Hattie hauls off and marries Haystack Duggeler, which is a great surprise to one and all, but not nearly as much of a surprise as when Hattie closes her boarding and rooming house and goes to live in a little apartment with Haystack Duggeler up on Washington Heights.

It seems that she finds Haystack one frosty night sleeping in a hallway, after being around slightly mulled up for several weeks, and she takes him to her home and gets him a bath and a shave and a clean shirt and two boiled eggs and some toast and coffee and a

88

shot or two of rye whisky, all of which is greatly appreciated by Haystack, especially the rye whisky.

Then Haystack proposes marriage to her and takes a paralyzed oath that if she becomes his wife he will reform, so what with loving Haystack anyway, and with the fix commencing to request more dough off the boarding-and-rooming-house business than the business will stand, Hattie takes him at his word, and there you are.

The baseball writers are wondering what Manager Mac will say when he hears these tidings, but all Mac says is that Haystack cannot possibly be any worse married than he is single-o, and then Mac has the club office send the happy couple a little paper money to carry them over the winter.

Well, what happens but a great change comes over Haystack Duggeler. He stops bending his elbow and helps Hattie cook and wash the dishes, and holds her hand when they are in the movies, and speaks of his love for her several times a week, and Hattie is as happy as nine dollars' worth of lettuce. Manager Mac is so delighted at the change in Haystack that he has the club office send over more paper money, because Mac knows that with Haystack in shape he is sure of twenty-five games, and maybe the pennant.

In late February, Haystack reports to the training camp down South still as sober as some judges, and the other ballplayers are so impressed by the change in him that they admit him to their poker game again. But of course it is too much to expect a man to alter his entire course of living all at once, and it is not long before Haystack discovers four nines in his hand on his own deal and breaks up the game.

He brings Baseball Hattie with him to the camp, and this is undoubtedly a slight mistake, as it seems the old rumor about her boarding-and-rooming-house business gets around among the ever-loving wives of the other players, and they put on a large chill for her. In fact, you will think Hattie has the smallpox.

Naturally, Baseball Hattie feels the frost, but she never lets on, as it seems she runs into many bigger and better frosts than this in her time. Then Haystack Duggeler notices it, and it seems that it makes him a little peevish toward Baseball Hattie, and in fact it is said that he gives her a slight pasting one night in their room, partly because she has no better social standing and partly because he is commencing to cop a few sneaks on the local corn now and then, and Hattie chides him for same.

Well, about this time it appears that Baseball Hattie discovers that she is going to have a baby, and as soon as she recovers from her astonishment, she decides that it is to be a boy who will be a great baseball player, maybe a pitcher, although Hattie admits she is willing to compromise on a good second baseman.

She also decides that his name is to be Derrill Duggeler, after his paw, as it seems Derrill is Haystack's real name, and he is only called Haystack because he claims he once made a living stacking hay, although the general opinion is that all he ever stacks is cards.

It is really quite remarkable what a belt Hattie gets out of the idea of having this baby, though Haystack is not excited about the matter. He is not paying much attention to Baseball Hattie by now, except to give her a slight pasting now and then, but Hattie is so happy about the baby that she does not mind these pastings.

90

Haystack Duggeler meets up with Armand Fibleman along in midsummer. By this time, Haystack discovers horse racing and is always making bets on horses, and naturally he is generally broke, and then I commence running into him in different spots with Armand Fibleman, who is now betting higher than a cat's back on baseball games.

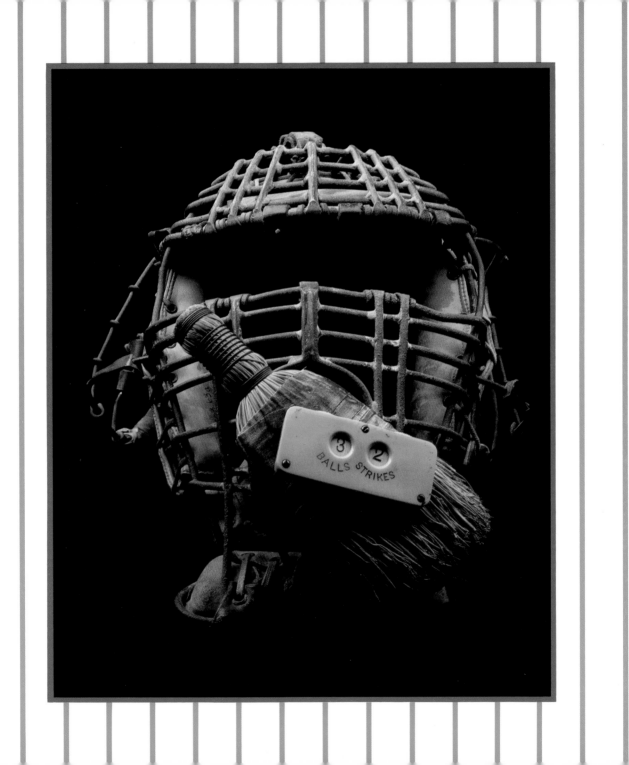

runyon

It is late August, and the Giants are fighting for the front end of the league, and an important series with Brooklyn is coming up, and everybody knows that Haystack Duggeler will work in anyway two games of the series, as Haystack can generally beat Brooklyn just by throwing his glove on the mound. There is no doubt but what he has the old Indian sign on Brooklyn, and the night before the first game, which he is sure to work, the gamblers along Broadway are making the Giants two-to-one favorites to win the game.

This same night before the game, Baseball Hattie is home in her little apartment on Washington Heights waiting for Haystack to come in and eat a delicious dinner of pigs' knuckles and sauerkraut, which she personally prepares for him. In fact, she hurries home right after the ball game to get this delicacy ready, because Haystack tells her he will surely come home this particular night, although Hattie knows he is never better than even money to keep his word about anything.

But sure enough, in he comes while the pigs' knuckles and sauerkraut are still piping hot, and Baseball Hattie is surprised to see Armand Fibleman with him, as she knows Armand backwards and forwards and does not care much for him, at that. However, she can say the same thing about four million other characters in this town, so she makes Armand welcome, and they sit down and put on the pigs' knuckles and sauerkraut together, and a pleasant time is enjoyed by one and all. In fact, Baseball Hattie puts herself out to entertain Armand Fibleman, because he is the first guest Haystack ever brings home.

Well, Armand Fibleman can be very pleasant when he wishes, and he speaks very nicely to Hattie. Naturally, he sees that Hattie is expecting, and in fact he will have to be blind not to see it, and he seems greatly interested in this matter and asks Hattie many questions, and Hattie is delighted to find somebody to talk to about what is coming off with her, as Haystack will never listen to any of her remarks on the subject.

So Armand Fibleman gets to hear all about Baseball Hattie's son, and how he is to be a great baseball player, and Armand says is that so, and how nice, and all this and that, until Haystack Duggeler speaks up as follows, and to wit:

"Oh, dag-gone her son!" Haystack says. "It is going to be a girl, anyway, so let us dismiss this topic and get down to business. Hat," he says, "you fan yourself into the kitchen and wash the dishes, while Armand and me talk."

So Hattie goes into the kitchen, leaving Haystack and Armand sitting there talking, and what are they talking about but a proposition for Haystack to let the Brooklyn club beat him the next day so Armand Fibleman can take the odds and clean up a nice little gob of money, which he is to split with Haystack.

Hattie can hear every word they say, as the kitchen is next door to the dining room where they are sitting, and at first she thinks they are joking, because at this time nobody ever even as much as thinks of skulduggery in baseball, or anyway, not much.

It seems that at first Haystack is not in favor of the idea, but Armand Fibleman keeps mentioning money that Haystack owes him for bets on the horse races, and he asks Haystack how he expects to continue betting on the races without fresh money, and Armand also speaks of the great injustice that is being done Haystack by the Giants in not paying him twice the salary he is getting, and how the loss of one or two games is by no means such a great calamity.

Well, finally Baseball Hattie hears Haystack say all right, but he wishes a thousand

93

runyon

dollars then and there as a guarantee, and Armand Fibleman says this is fine, and they will go downtown and he will get the money at once, and now Hattie realizes that maybe they are in earnest, and she pops out of the kitchen and speaks as follows:

"Gentlemen," Hattie says, "you seem to be sober, but I guess you are drunk. If you are not drunk, you must both be daffy to think of such a thing as finagling around with a baseball game."

"Hattie," Haystack says, "kindly close your trap and go back in the kitchen, or I will give you a bust in the nose."

And with this he gets up and reaches for his hat, and Armand Fibleman gets up, too, and Hattie says like this:

"Why, Haystack," she says, "you are not really serious in this matter, are you?"

"Of course I am serious," Haystack says. "I am sick and tired of pitching for starvation wages, and besides, I will win a lot of games later on to make up for the one I lose tomorrow. Say," he says, "these Brooklyn bums may get lucky tomorrow and knock me loose from my pants, anyway, no matter what I do, so what difference does it make?"

"Haystack," Baseball Hattie says, "I know you are a liar and a drunkard and a cheat and no account generally, but nobody can tell me you will sink so low as to purposely toss off a ball game. Why, Haystack, baseball is always on the level. It is the most honest game in all this world. I guess you are just ribbing me, because you know how much I love it."

"Dry up!" Haystack says to Hattie. "Furthermore, do not expect me home again tonight. But anyway, dry up."

"Look, Haystack," Hattie says, "I am going to have a son. He is your son and my son, and he is going to be a great ballplayer when he grows up, maybe a greater pitcher than you are, though I hope and trust he is not left-handed. He will have your name. If they find out you toss off a game for money, they will throw you out of baseball and you will be disgraced. My son will be known as the son of a crook, and what chance will he have in baseball? Do you think I am going to allow you to do this to him, and to the game that keeps me from going nutty for marrying you?"

Naturally, Haystack Duggeler is greatly offended by Hattie's crack about her son being maybe a greater pitcher than he is, and he is about to take steps, when Armand Fibleman stops him. Armand Fibleman is commencing to be somewhat alarmed by Baseball Hattie's attitude, and he gets to thinking that he hears that people in her delicate condition are often irresponsible, and he fears that she may blow a whistle on this enterprise without realizing what she is doing. So he undertakes a few soothing remarks to her.

"Why, Hattie," Armand Fibleman says, "nobody can possibly find out about this little matter, and Haystack will have enough money to send your son to college, if his markers at the race track do not take it all. Maybe you better lie down and rest awhile," Armand says.

But Baseball Hattie does not as much as look at Armand, though she goes on talking to Haystack. "They always find out thievery, Haystack," she says, "especially when you are dealing with a fink like Fibleman. If you deal with him once, you will have to deal with him again and again, and he will be the first to holler copper on you, because he is a stool pigeon in his heart."

"Haystack," Armand Fibleman says, "I think we better be going."

"Haystack," Hattie says, "you can go out of here and stick up somebody or commit a robbery or a murder, and I will still welcome you back and stand by you. But if you are

95

going out to steal my son's future, I advise you not to go."

"Dry up!" Haystack says. "I am going."

"All right, Haystack," Hattie says, very calm. "But just step into the kitchen with me and let me say one little word to you by yourself, and then I will say no more."

Well, Haystack Duggeler does not care for even just one little word more, but Armand Fibleman wishes to get this disagreeable scene over with, so he tells Haystack to let her have her word, and Haystack goes into the kitchen with Hattie, and Armand cannot hear what is said, as she speaks very low, but he hears Haystack laugh heartily and then Haystack comes out of the kitchen, still laughing, and tells Armand he is ready to go.

As they start for the door, Baseball Hattie outs with a long-nosed .38-caliber Colt's revolver, and goes root-a-toot-toot with it, and the next thing anybody knows, Haystack is on the floor yelling bloody murder, and Armand Fibleman is leaving the premises without bothering to open the door. In fact, the landlord afterwards talks some of suing Haystack Duggeler because of the damage Armand Fibleman does to the door. Armand himself afterwards admits that when he slows down for a breather a couple of miles down Broadway he finds splinters stuck all over him.

Well, the doctors come, and the gendarmes come, and there is great confusion, especially as Baseball Hattie is sobbing so she can scarcely make a statement, and Haystack Duggeler is so sure he is going to die that he can not think of anything to say except oh-oh-oh, but finally the landlord remembers seeing Armand leave with his door, and everybody starts questioning Hattie about this until she confesses that Armand is all right, and that he tries to bribe Haystack to toss off a ball game, and that she then suddenly finds herself with a revolver in her hand, and everything goes black before her eyes, and she can

96

remember no more until somebody is sticking a bottle of smelling salts under her nose.

Naturally, the newspaper reporters put two and two together, and what they make of it is that Hattie tries to plug Armand Fibleman for his rascally offer, and that she misses Armand and gets Haystack, and right away Baseball Hattie is a great heroine, and Haystack is a great hero, though nobody thinks to ask Haystack how he stands on the bribe proposition, and he never brings it up himself.

And nobody will ever offer Haystack any more bribes, for after the doctors get through with him he is shy a left arm from the shoulder down, and he will never pitch a baseball again, unless he learns to pitch right-handed.

The newspapers make quite a lot of Baseball Hattie protecting the fair name of baseball. The National League plays a benefit game for Haystack Duggeler and presents him with a watch and a purse of twenty-five thousand dollars, which Baseball Hattie grabs away from him, saying it is for her son, while Armand Fibleman is in bad with one and all.

Baseball Hattie and Haystack Duggeler move to the Pacific Coast, and this is all there is to the story, except that one day some years ago, and not long before he passes away in Los Angeles, a respectable grocer, I run into Haystack when he is in New York on a business trip, and I say to him like this:

"Haystack," I say, "it is certainly a sin and a shame that Hattie misses Armand Fibleman that night and puts you on the shelf. The chances are that but for this little accident you will hang up one of the greatest pitching records in the history of baseball. Personally," I say, "I never see a better left-handed pitcher."

"Look," Haystack says. "Hattie does not miss Fibleman. It is a great newspaper story and saves my name, but truth is she hits just where she aims. When she calls me into the kitchen before I start out with Fibleman, she shows me a revolver I never before know she has, and says to me, 'Haystack,' she says, 'if you leave with this weasel on the errand you mention, I am going to fix you so you will never make another wrong move with your pitching arm. I am going to shoot it off for you.'

"I laugh heartily," Haystack says. "I think she is kidding me, but I find out different. By the way," Haystack says, "I afterwards learn that long before I meet her, Hattie works for three years in a shooting gallery at Coney Island. She is really a remarkable broad," Haystack says.

I guess I forget to state that the day Baseball Hattie is at the Polo Grounds she is watching the new kid sensation of the big leagues, Derrill Duggeler, shut out Brooklyn with three hits.

He is a wonderful young left-hander.

contributors

W(illiam) P(atrick) KINSELLA (1935-) is an honored member of the Literary Hall of Fame. His novel *Shoeless Joe* "hit the ball out-of-the-park," and was later made into the movie *Field of Dreams.* He owned a pizza parlor and drove a cab before he found his true calling, to write wonderfully entertaining tales "that make people laugh and cry." A native of Canada, he writes from his home in British Columbia. "How I Got My Nickname" was published in 1984 as part of an anthology of his stories titled *The Thrill of the Grass.*

JAMES THURBER (1894-1961) was a charter member of that college-educated coterie of diners who broke their bread around the Algonquin Roundtable. Thurber began his career as a *New Yorker* cartoonist and used his skill to decorate his stories with hilarous illustrations. Often compared to Mark Twain for his biting wit, he claimed never to have read a work by that esteemed gentleman of letters. "The Secret Life of Walter Mitty," *The Male Animal,* and *My Life and Hard Times* are his best known works. "You Could Look It Up" was published in 1942.

NUNNALLY JOHNSON (1897-1977) was an award-winning screenwriter, director, and producer; his film credits shine like jewels in the crown of Hollywood's all star line-up. *The Grapes of Wrath, The Three Faces of Eve, The Man in the Grey Flannel Suit, How to Marry a Millionaire, Mr. Peabody and the Mermaid,* and *The World of Henry Orient* (based on his daughter Nora's novel), form only the pedestal of this showman's monumental contribution

to the silver screen. Life on the Coast was a far cry from his childhood beginnings in Columbus Georgia. He began his writing career as a cub reporter for his hometown paper, the *Columbus Enquirer Sun,* graduated to the *Brooklyn Daily Eagle,* the *New York Herald Tribune,* and the *New York Post,* and was inspired by city-life to write his first short story "The Rollicking God," in 1924.

EDNA FERBER (1887-1968) cast her canny reporter's eye upon the heartland of America. With bestsellers such as *Cimarron, Giant,* and the Pulitzer prize-winning *So Big,* she left us a literary montage of life during the first half of the twentieth century. As a young girl from Kalamazoo, she adored the theater, whether played on the paddle steamers of the Mississippi, the setting for her novel *Show Boat,* or on the boards of Broadway, the backdrop for her smash hits *Dinner at Eight* and *Stage Door.* "Bush League Hero," one of a multitude of her charming short stories, was first published circa 1910.

DAMON RUNYON (1884-1946), American journalist and playwright, is renowned for his marvelous short stories. Written in New Yorkese, littered with streetwise insights, and washed down with a slice of cheesecake from Mindy's, his best-loved tales of the city, such as "Guys and Dolls," "Little Miss Marker," "Butch Minds the Baby," and "Dancing Dan's Christmas," lit the literary landscape like a marqee on Broadway's Great White Way. "Baseball Hattie" was published in 1936.

100

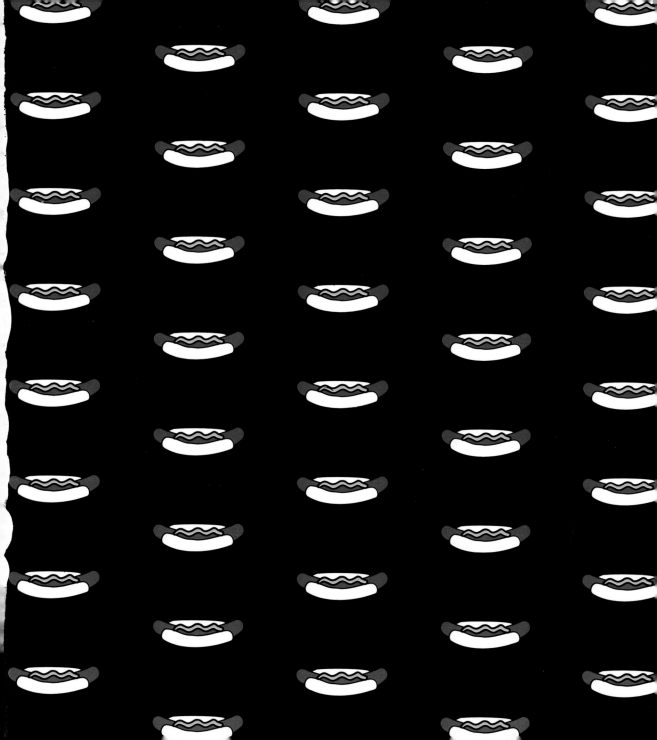

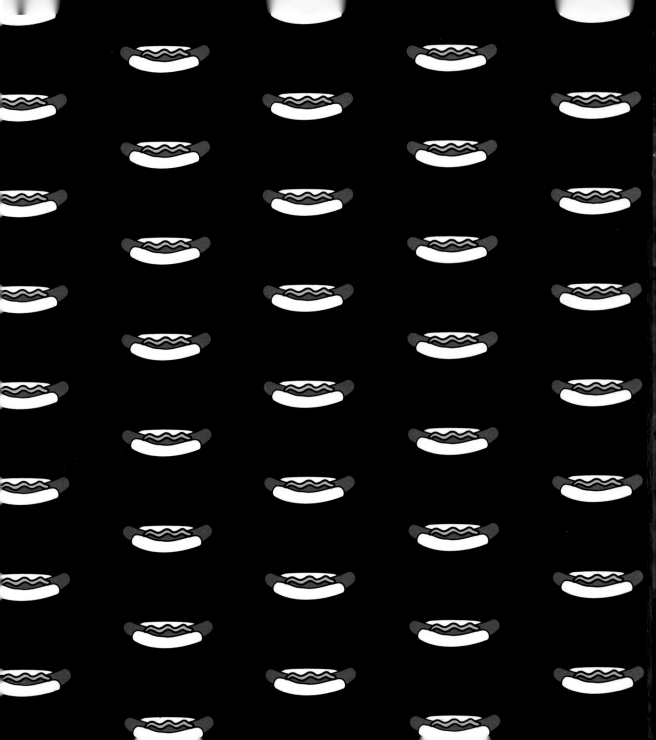